Sti

*Pop...   ...rlequin Blaze author
Debbi Rawlins keeps readers in the saddle
with her continuing miniseries*

Made in Montana

*Since the McAllisters opened a dude ranch
catering to single women,
the sleepy town of Blackfoot Falls
has gotten a lot more interesting....*

Get your hands on a hot cowboy with

#701 Barefoot Blue Jean Night
(August 2012)

#713 Own the Night
(October 2012)

#725 On a Snowy Christmas Night
(December 2012)

#736 You're Still the One
(February 2013)

#744 No One Needs to Know
(April 2013)

#753 From This Moment On
(June 2013)

*And remember,
the sexiest cowboys are Made in Montana!*

Dear Reader,

Like the pesky relative who comes for the weekend but never seems to leave, I've set up shop in Blackfoot Falls and I'm not going anywhere! This time I want to tell you about mysterious Annie Sheridan, who arrived in town two years ago and runs Safe Haven Animal Sanctuary.

Annie first appeared in Jesse and Shea's book, *On a Snowy Christmas Night*. I didn't know right away that she'd have her own story. But she was different, intriguing, not someone you'd expect to find living a solitary life in the middle of nowhere. So who was she?

The pieces fell together quickly. Tucker Brennan sprang to life in a flash. This sinfully handsome gentleman rancher from Dallas is interested in a lot more than funding Safe Haven. He knows Annie isn't who she appears to be.

There are secrets and lies to expose, a wrong to put right, and Tucker's just the man to topple Annie's house of cards. What he didn't count on was falling for her.

I hope you all enjoy this tall Texan, especially when he's in well-worn jeans…and nothing else. Annie couldn't resist him, and frankly, neither could I!

All my best,

Debbi Rawlins

No One Needs to Know

—

Debbi Rawlins

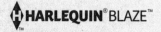

ISBN-13: 978-0-373-79748-6

NO ONE NEEDS TO KNOW

HARLEQUIN®

Printed in U.S.A.

™ www.Harlequin.com

ABOUT THE AUTHOR

Debbi Rawlins grew up in the country with no fast-food drive-throughs or nearby neighbors, so one might think as a kid she'd be dazzled by the bright lights of the city, the allure of the unfamiliar. Not so. She loved Westerns in movies and books, and her first crush was on a cowboy—okay, he was an actor in the role of a cowboy, but she was only eleven, so it counts. It was in Houston, Texas, where she first started writing for Harlequin, and now, more than fifty books later, she has her own ranch... of sorts. Instead of horses, she has four dogs, five cats, a trio of goats and free-range cattle keeping her on her toes on a few acres in gorgeous rural Utah. And of course, the deer and elk are always welcome.

Books by Debbi Rawlins

HARLEQUIN BLAZE

To get the inside scoop on Harlequin Blaze and its talented writers, be sure to check out blazeauthors.com.

1

FROM HER PERCH ON THE PORCH railing at the Sundance ranch, Annie Sheridan took what she called a memory shot. If she'd had her beloved old Nikon she'd have pulled it out and centered the lens on the familiar faces of her hosts, but the spectacular sunset against the Rocky Mountains would have been the star. Only to the casual observer, though, which Annie most definitely was not.

She'd become an expert at the art of watching from a distance. It didn't even bother her that much, not anymore. Two years into exile, she'd grown used to being the strange woman who ran the Safe Haven large-animal sanctuary, the one who never came to parties unless there was something her shelter needed—a favor, a donation, an adoptive home. Of course everyone in Blackfoot Falls knew who she was, and it would have stunned her if the residents of the small town hadn't made up at least a dozen stories to explain her hermit ways.

No one, she was sure, would ever come close to the truth.

She sipped from her glass of white zinfandel, a rare treat along with the scrumptious steak and baked potato she'd had earlier. The last time she'd eaten at a party was…in another life.

That sobering thought had her off the railing and heading toward Barbara McAllister and the cluster of family that surrounded the Sundance matriarch. If Annie let herself yearn for anything these days—outside of more money for Safe Haven—it was the friendship of this clan. The three brothers—Cole, Jesse and Trace—were always willing to lend a hand during an emergency. Jesse had saved many a poor animal's life, or given a horse or a llama or a potbellied pig a new home with his rescue airlifts.

Then there was Rachel and her boyfriend, Matt, so giddily in love. In the past six months two of the three McAllister brothers had hooked up. And now with Rachel taken, that only left Trace on the loose. Something the Sundance dude ranch guests, all of them single women in their twenties or early thirties, were trying to remedy.

Rachel had made several attempts at befriending her, though Annie had kept her distance. But boundary lines that had once been set in stone were becoming more flexible.

"Are you getting ready to leave?"

Annie smiled at Jesse's girlfriend. The whole reason Annie was socializing at all was due to unassuming, crazy-generous Shea. Taking a break from her high-security job as a computer programmer, she'd come to Montana over the Christmas holidays to help at Safe Haven. But she'd come back to Blackfoot Falls because of Jesse. That she'd turned out to be the sanctuary's most influential volunteer and backer was a miracle.

Annie sighed with real regret as she nodded. "I have chores."

"Need help?"

"Not from you, although thanks for offering. You stay right here and enjoy yourself with that man of yours."

Shea blushed as she slipped her hands into the pockets of her dark gray trousers. "I'm glad you stayed so long. Jesse said you've never had dinner here before."

"You know how things are. Always something to do, what with every female animal at the shelter pregnant."

Shea laughed. "Not every one."

Annie set her glass on a big tray, knowing no one would mind that she didn't stay to clean up. "It's been a nice party."

"It has," Shea said, with more than a little surprise in her voice. "I usually hate parties. Never know what to say. But with the McAllisters it's different." She leaned in a little closer and lowered her voice. "Yesterday, I talked to Sadie from the Watering Hole for almost half an hour."

"Whoa, look at you, Shea. You haven't even lived here a full month yet and you're already one of the in crowd."

"Jesse tries to include me in things because he knows I'm oblivious," she said in that matter-of-fact tone that still made Annie smile. "Not with gossip, though. He doesn't do that."

Perhaps because he'd heard his name, the man in question sidled up to Shea and snuck his arm across her shoulders, but kept his gaze on Annie.

"I'm flying out to Missoula on Tuesday," Jesse said, "so you might want to put together a shopping list."

She perked up because it was about a hundred miles to Missoula, and she could get things there that weren't available in a small town like Blackfoot Falls or even the bigger Kalispell. Northwestern Montana was gorgeous, but it was mostly land and lakes and mountains. "I'll get on that tomorrow."

"With all that loot you two have been raking in," Jesse said, "it'll be hard to decide what to buy first."

Annie smiled at his teasing. He was the only other person who knew how much of the influx of money had come either directly from Shea or from donations she'd wrangled. Annie pulled her keys out of her pocket. "Trust me, most of it is spent and we had no trouble doing it. Unbelievable how many things need replacing or fixing at that sorry shelter."

"Your cabin, for instance?" Shea said.

"My cabin is fine, thanks." Annie addressed Jesse again, wanting to change the subject quickly. "I'll send a list home with Shea." She looked at her. "I'll see you tomorrow morning?"

"Of course."

Annie fiddled with her keys as she backed up in the direction of her truck. "Great. See you then." She said quick goodbyes to most of the McAllisters along with many thanks, but before they could even try to convince her to stick around for dessert she climbed into her old green pickup.

No matter what she did or how long she left the windows open, the cab always smelled like horses. She didn't mind. Horses had been a comfort to her all her life, and even though they were an amazing amount of work, especially this time of year, she couldn't have wished for better company.

Horses didn't care that she was on the run, that she'd messed up her life beyond repair. They loved her, anyway.

It didn't take long to reach Safe Haven, and the first thing she did was check on the animals in the stable. She had an abandoned stallion that was starting to pick up some weight and get a little shine to his coat, and she added some grain to his feed trough. She spent longer checking on the mares, both of them with full teats but only in the prep stage of foaling, so there was time.

An hour later, she was finished with the barn chores and walked the couple hundred feet to the cabin everyone was so obsessed with. Inside, the overhead light sputtered to life, giving her a shadowed view of her home.

No, it wasn't much, but it served its purpose. She could run her computer, plus she had a coffeemaker, a microwave, a toaster oven and a minifridge. Hell, she'd lived for years with less at the Columbia University dorms. The tiny claustrophobic bathroom wasn't a big deal anymore, though she missed having a tub. But the shower got reasonably hot, and she'd replaced the cracked mirror. And the toilet…well, that could use replacing, too. But not until the emergency supplies were stocked and the tractor had a new engine.

Once upstairs in her loft, she turned on the lamp by her bed, and only then realized she should have changed out of her good jeans and one nice shirt before she'd done chores. No use worrying about that now, though. It was late for her, and the alarm would go off before first light, so she pulled on her nightshirt, and by nine-thirty she was under the covers reading a paperback thriller.

A chapter in, her eyelids started sinking. Thankfully, sleep wasn't hard to come by anymore. The key was to keep herself in a constant state of exhaustion. She'd become an expert at that, too.

FOR THE SECOND TIME IN AN HOUR, Tucker Brennan found himself more focused on the view of the stables outside his window than the business at hand. There were several wranglers busy with chores, just like on the rest of his ranch. He would have preferred being out there building up a sweat instead of sitting in his office, filling his day with the business of running the Rocking B.

His Monday morning had gotten off to a rough start. He'd slept through his alarm, then spilled coffee on his lap during breakfast. Maybe he should have gone out last night. There were a number of women he could've called who wouldn't have minded a last-minute invitation. But it was never that easy, was it?

"There's a fundraiser for City of Hope next month."

Tucker turned his chair so he faced his personal assistant, who was seconds into an eye roll. Darren smoothed over the near-gaff by clearing his throat. Tucker didn't let his own frustration show, knowing full well this probably wasn't the first time Darren had brought up this particular agenda item. Or the second.

"It's at the McDermott?"

"Yes. Black tie," Darren said. "The Dallas Symphony Orchestra will be performing before the gala."

Tucker clicked over to his May calendar where Darren had already highlighted the date. He had three other formal events in May and the thought of another one didn't appeal. "Send them a check, please. Personal."

"Match last year's?"

It had been sizable. "Yes."

They continued to go down the list of requests, which seemed to grow exponentially year by year. While Darren did most of the correspondence concerning the ranch operations, Tucker liked to write personal messages where it counted. Like the one to an old warhorse of a rancher from Idaho who was about to retire. With no heir, he was going to auction off sixty thousand acres, along with his cattle and horses and all his equipment, and Tucker meant to purchase a great deal of the stock.

He barely acknowledged Darren leaving the office and

set to work composing a letter to the rancher, handwritten, just like the old days, because Cotton and his late wife, Lula, had sent out Christmas letters every year until she'd passed away in 2009.

Just as Tucker started the second paragraph, a notification popped up on his computer. He went to delete the intrusion with one quick click, but the words stopped him.

He saved his screen and switched to Google, where he'd set up dozens of alerts a year ago, having no faith whatsoever that he'd ever hit pay dirt. He'd gotten hundreds of hits because there wasn't anything all that unique about the chosen keywords, but he never skipped a one. This particular alert was for the name *Ann,* even though the object of his search had been born Leanna Warner. The other keywords were *horses* and *fundraising.*

Tucker wasn't even sure why he'd bothered, because that was too close to Leanna's true history. But he'd been thorough and he never let himself get his hopes up. He clicked on the link.

A blonde woman sat in the corner of a photograph. She wasn't looking at the camera, but to her left. Saving the photo, he brought up the Warner file he kept under a separate password. He'd gathered everything he could about the woman a year ago, right after his brother, Christian, had given up his tough-guy act and confessed that he'd been hoodwinked…. By a slick fundraiser who was tall and slender and had a face that made men do foolish things.

Leanna was a card-carrying member of the Association of Fundraising Professionals with an office in Park Slope. She'd started out with a big firm, eventually opening her own office.

She and Christian had done quite well building up a sizable fund to benefit a number of charities. Only, none of the dividends reached the account. Instead, the investment profits had disappeared. Vanished. So had Leanna Warner, but only after the New York district attorney's office, acting on a complaint, had gone after Christian.

While there was a lot of circumstantial evidence putting the money in Christian's hands, there was no proof, no paper trail. Not that the D.A.'s office had stopped looking. They had made it clear Christian would remain a person of interest until they found Leanna and took her testimony. In the two years since the embezzlement, including the year Tucker had been conducting his own investigation, there hadn't been a single clue as to her whereabouts.

Tucker still wasn't sure there was one now. The pictures he had of Leanna showed an elegant, sophisticated New Yorker. She'd been one of the Manhattan hungry, seeking her fortune and status among the elite. If her plan had been to cut and run, she'd done herself a disservice. With her looks and the confidence she displayed on the two videos he'd found of her, she could have gone far.

Greed had a way of making fools of even the most promising.

Trouble was, he couldn't be sure that the woman, identified simply as Annie, was Leanna Warner. If she'd only turned a little more toward the camera... Besides, this woman looked as if she'd been born in Western gear.

He ran one of the old videos and froze it when he had a decent view of her profile. He pulled up the two images so they were side by side on his monitor. For a long time, he just flicked his gaze from one to the other, and dammit, there were similarities. The odds were not high that he'd found the missing Warner, but it would drive him crazy not to know for sure. More importantly, he owed this to Christian.

Tucker didn't have to look up the number for George Morgan, a family friend who also happened to be a private investigator in New York. He'd been on the case from the moment Christian had told Tucker about Leanna Warner, and while George had found out about her past, he'd had no luck finding the woman herself.

"Tucker. It's been a while."

"Too long," Tucker said, leaning back in his chair, staring at the new picture as if her position would change if he looked hard enough. "I'm calling about Leanna Warner."

George took a second. "Did something happen?"

"Maybe. I might have uncovered a picture, although I wouldn't count on it. If it is her, she's living in a flyspeck town in northern Montana, working at an animal sanctuary."

"You want me to go check things out." It wasn't a question.

"I'd like that, yes."

"I'm slammed at the moment but I can go in a couple of weeks." Met with silence, George added, "Or I can recommend a couple of other investigators if you'd like."

That changed things. Tucker hadn't realized how invested he was in finding Warner until this photo had cropped up. Locating her might not solve all the issues he had with his brother, certainly wouldn't fix things between Christian and their mother, but it would be a significant start. "Maybe I'll fly out there myself. It's probably a fool's errand, but if it is her, I'll make damn sure she doesn't run again."

"You know, there's no guarantee that bringing her to the district attorney will be enough to clear Christian's name."

"I know." Tucker stared out the window, trying to organize his thoughts. "I won't be hasty. I'll take a look around. See if I can dig up something tying her to the money."

"I don't know.… Sure it can't wait two weeks?"

He smiled. "I won't do anything risky. In fact, I have

the perfect cover. My foundation funds sanctuaries and shelters."

"Or you can have a look, confirm it's her and, while you wait for me, take some time to go fishing. Montana has some great streams and lakes."

Tucker laughed.

George did, too. "I know. What was I thinking? You're so much like your old man. He never took time off, either."

"Listen, do me a favor. When you can, dust off those Warner files, huh? It's been a while. Let's see if we missed a connection somewhere along the way."

"That I can do fairly quickly."

After they hung up, Tucker looked at his April calendar.

It was jammed, of course. The Rocking B ranch, started on a shoestring by his adoptive grandfather, built into an empire by his late step-father, was over 500,000 acres. They raised cattle, horses and crops, and there were twelve working oil wells on 160,000 acres of backcountry land. Although he had managers to handle the day-to-day business, the buck stopped with Tucker.

It wasn't easy for him to make the trip himself, but he'd manage. If he rearranged his schedule, he could go the following Monday. That time frame would give him a chance to refresh himself on Leanna's history and find out what he could about Safe Haven and the town of Blackfoot Falls.

He called Darren in, and they began the work of shuffling appointments. There wouldn't be any problem, except for one—he dedicated Tuesday nights to dinner with his mother. If he flew out Monday, he doubted he'd be back in time.

Irene lived on the ranch in a private suite of rooms, but they didn't cross paths that often. She had her own social circle that kept her reasonably busy, but she was still grieving for her husband, who'd died eighteen months ago.

Tucker spent his weekends in Dallas proper taking care of social obligations, and worked the rest of the week at the ranch. She probably wouldn't say much, but of all the things Irene did, she most looked forward to their weekly dinner. He hated disappointing her, but it couldn't be helped.

While Darren went through item after item, Tucker kept staring at the pictures he'd pulled back up on his computer. He might want to blame his younger brother for being so gullible, but that didn't mean Tucker wouldn't help him clear his name. There was more at stake here. Christian had gotten the short straw when they'd been children, and while Tucker's own guilt was great, it was nothing compared to their mother's.

He couldn't afford to wait for George. Tucker needed to see this "Annie" for himself. And if she was the woman who'd left Christian holding the bag for her crimes, delivering her to justice might help bring his erstwhile family together again.

AS ANNIE SIPPED HER COFFEE, she checked the big blackboard above her desk. On it were the days of the week, the scheduled volunteers, appointments, deadlines…basically her life in chalk.

Mondays were always fun, at least in the early afternoon when Melanie Knowles brought a group of high school students to volunteer. Melanie had convinced the principal and the school board to give the students academic credits for their participation. Each time a group arrived in the small yellow bus, they had an hour of instruction—everything from animal husbandry to money management—before being assigned tasks.

Melanie and the students had even started a major project on their own that would benefit the shelter for years to come.

Thank goodness, because Safe Haven wasn't in nearly good enough financial shape to handle anything outside the basics of feeding and caring for the animals. But at least they'd made significant headway by turning the operation into a not-for-profit organization that was finally eligible for grant money and more substantial donations. All thanks to Shea. She'd helped Annie with the paperwork, but her participation meant much more. Shea was the name and face of Safe Haven.

Just remembering the days before Annie had asked Shea to serve as Safe Haven's chairman of the board made Annie tense. The future of the sanctuary had been at stake. Annie couldn't use her real name on any government document. Since she was an unpaid volunteer, she wasn't noted at all.

The rest of the board positions had been filled with longtime residents of Blackfoot Falls, and they were one hell of an ornery bunch. Their first meeting would be next week, and wasn't that going to be a corker. Annie would be there to run things—Shea had made her promise—but with an official and legal board of directors, Safe Haven would continue even if Annie had to disappear in a hurry.

That thought sent her mood plummeting. Better get busy before she had too much time to brood.

It wasn't light out yet, but she'd have to start the first round of feeding shortly, so she booted up her computer and checked her email. She didn't get much. A few volunteers liked to keep in touch between visits, some ebills had to be slotted for payment. Shea had sent pictures of yesterday's party that she'd posted on the Sundance website.

The fourth one nearly stopped her heart.

It was a picture of her. For anyone to see. Including the New York district attorney.

2

TUCKER WAS ALREADY IN THE sunroom, waiting for his mother to join him for lunch. He never minded spending time with her, but he wished he could do something more to lift her spirits.

Finding Leanna Warner would help. Irene wanted so badly to bring Christian back into her life that Tucker would do just about anything he could to make that happen. Proving Christian's innocence was no guarantee that he'd see past the pain of being abandoned as a child and give his mother and Tucker another chance. But it was Tucker's best shot.

Tucker had gone through his own pain and doubt during his parents' bitter divorce, but he'd been the lucky one. He'd ended up with his mother, a man he admired as his new father and a legacy of wealth and privilege to live up to. Christian had been the bargaining chip for Rory Andrews to grant Irene her divorce. She'd never dreamed that Rory would vanish, would subject Christian to a nomadic life following the horse-racing circuit and running from debts.

That Christian had gone to college and received his master's in finance was a testament to hard work and determination, because there'd been no support from his dad.

Now, to have this cloud of suspicion over his reputation was another kick in the teeth Christian didn't deserve.

Every time Tucker thought of the grief Leanna Warner had brought down on his family it angered him further, but he'd never been one to act rashly. By the time he turned that woman in, he'd make damn sure his brother would be exonerated completely.

Irene entered the room with her head high, and a smile on her face. It was all for show, but sometimes he thought the facade was the only thing keeping her going. That and hope.

THE MORNING WENT BY IN FITS and starts, and Shea was late. Her phone was going straight to voice mail, which meant she probably hadn't remembered to turn it on again. Annie had gone back to the computer several times, just to make sure she wasn't freaking out over nothing, but she wasn't. Her picture, along with her first name being associated with Safe Haven, was plenty to worry about. Shea would know how many hits the site had logged, and that page in particular. A high number would be more reason to run as quickly as possible. A low number meant it was far less risky for Annie to stay.

God, she wanted to stay.

The irony wasn't lost on her. She'd been so intent on becoming a mover and shaker in Manhattan that she'd gotten herself into the worst trouble she could imagine. Now, she was desperate to live in a cabin that made her first New York apartment look roomy, and had fallen in love with a life of pitching hay and nursing everything from piglets to Brahma bulls. But she'd better stop romanticizing the sanctuary and her life, because that would make running even harder.

"Annie? Can I ride Candy Cane after class?"

Shaken out of her slide toward panic, she smiled at one of her favorite students—a small girl for a senior—who was deeply infatuated with horses. "You have a ride home?"

Stephanie nodded. "My mom said I could stay for an hour if it's okay with you."

"You bet. Candy needs a little exercise."

The girl ran back to the work of mucking out one of the birthing stalls as Annie heard a car crunching over the gravel driveway. Her heart beat furiously as Shea parked her truck.

"Sorry I'm late. I ran into Doc Yardley and we got to talking. But I remembered to bring the—"

Annie grabbed the bag of medicine from Shea's outstretched hand. "I need to speak to you," she said. "Inside. I'll be right there."

Shea's expression had gone from pleasant to worried, but instead of shooting back questions, she simply closed the truck door behind her and headed for the cabin.

Annie trotted to Melanie, who was helping one of the kids distribute feed to the goats. "Can you watch things for me? Something's come up."

Melanie, who had once considered becoming a vet, agreed at once.

It struck Annie hard that she knew so much about this quiet woman who'd made such an impact at Safe Haven and with her students. In fact, Annie knew a great deal about many of the people in this quaint Montana town. She'd meant to avoid all this. To keep to herself. Getting involved hadn't been part of the plan, and this was why.

She forced a smile for Melanie, then turned, wanting to run to the cabin. But it wasn't that far, and she could use the extra minute to calm herself. Since she'd seen the picture, she'd worried about a million things that could go wrong, but she hadn't bothered to think through what she was going to tell Shea. As little as possible, yes, but where was the line?

Shea looked up from the kitchen area when Annie walked inside. She was making a fresh pot of coffee. Annie wished she had something stronger.

"What's wrong?"

"I need to ask you a favor."

"Okay."

Annie studied the woman she'd gotten too close to. "The picture you posted on the Sundance website, the one with me in it? I need you to take it down. Please."

Shea didn't react, not even a lift of her eyebrows. "All right," she said calmly as she sat in front of Annie's computer. Shea typed very quickly. Logging into the Sundance website, it took only a few clicks to find the photo and delete it.

Annie sighed with relief. "Did you put it up this morning?"

"No. Last night," Shea said, returning to the desktop picture of the corral at sunset. "Late. Just before midnight."

Twelve hours. Annie's face had been freely available for twelve hours, but then the odds of someone from her past checking out the Sundance dude ranch website were miniscule. She didn't think facial recognition had come far enough along to have identified her from her somewhat fuzzy profile. Still, the smart thing to do would be to get out. Now. Just in case. "Do you know how many hits that page had?"

Shea typed a bit more. "Eighteen."

Eighteen wasn't bad. Eighteen could be just folks from town and some of the guests.

"I won't do that again," Shea said. "I didn't realize you disliked having your picture taken. I apologize."

All Annie had to do was nod, and that would be that. Shea wouldn't pry or tell anyone, with the possible exception of Jesse. They'd chalk it up to Annie's reclusive ways.

But this was Shea, who had given her time, her skills, her money and her friendship without any expectations. She never overstepped, respecting Annie's privacy in every way. Which would make leaving her in the dark the easiest thing ever.

The ache in Annie's chest was no reason to talk, to say aloud the secrets she'd been holding close for so long. In her old life, she'd been anything but an introvert. And she'd never met a camera she hadn't liked. "I used to be a professional fundraiser," she said, and those few words, that small admission, revved up her heart rate again. Made her flush with heat and fear and relief.

Shea went to the coffeepot and took out two mugs from the cupboard above.

Annie closed her eyes and tried to calm herself. By the time Shea put both cups of coffee down, Annie felt ready to begin. "I was good at it. I liked the work, even after the economy tanked. I made raising money for good causes my personal crusade. Not just because I was paid to do it, but because I knew that even in the worst of times, when people donated it made them feel better."

"Your effectiveness hasn't diminished at all," Shea said. "I can't believe how fearless you are in approaching everyone you see and how favorably most of them respond."

"People want to help. Well, most people." Annie briefly closed her eyes. "There are also those who understand the motives behind charitable giving, and use that information to steal and destroy people's faith and good intentions."

"What are you saying?" Shea looked at her plainly, expecting the truth. She wasn't naive, although some people mistook her manner for innocence.

"I worked with a partner who turned out to be one of the bad guys. Unfortunately, I didn't realize he'd been embezzling funds until it was far too late to do anything."

"Oh, Annie," Shea whispered, and Annie had to turn away so she wouldn't tear up.

"I had to leave my home. My everything."

"Surely no one would believe you were involved. That's ridiculous."

"Oh, but they could." Annie thought the bitterness had left her, but it still simmered inside. "I found out secondhand that one of my clients felt something wasn't right and approached my partner. He wanted to withdraw the money from the fund and invest it himself. My partner gave him the runaround and the client went to the district attorney."

She set her cup aside, rubbed her hands together, then down her jeans. The cabin was so small, there was no room to pace, but she couldn't sit still. She pulled herself up until her butt was on the edge of the sturdy table she used for everything from sewing to eating, then began to squeeze the beveled wood with her hands.

"The story hit the papers with the allegation that my partner was responsible but I might be involved after the fact. It was only a matter of days before I'd be subpoenaed by the state to tell them what I knew. Unfortunately, that amounted to nothing. I was as shocked as anyone when I saw that money was missing. All of the investment profits had been siphoned off. The seed money was still there. I went to an attorney, a good friend from college, and he flat out told me that I'd better have something on my partner. With charities involved, he felt certain someone would go down, and it could very easily be me."

Annie flexed her hands and tried to relax her body along

with her speeding thoughts. She'd never intended to tell Shea so much. Only, she'd been holding on to her silence for so long it was easy to keep talking, to spill everything. But the next part...

The next part was hard to think about, let alone say out loud. Besides, she wanted Shea to continue working with Safe Haven. To continue being a friend. "I'm not proud of what I did, but all I could think to do was run."

Shea sipped her coffee, clearly in thinking-things-through mode. When she looked at Annie again, her blue-gray eyes showed only concern. "I'm so sorry you had to go through that. It must be horribly difficult. Do you have a large family?"

"Mom, Dad, my younger sister. I left them a letter explaining so they wouldn't think I was dead. But I can't call."

"You must miss them."

Annie sighed. "Every day." She jumped down from the table and looked Shea in the eye. "Please, you have to keep this between us."

"Of course."

"Thank you." Annie maintained eye contact, hoping Shea understood that meant not telling Jesse. "And thanks for taking down the picture without even asking why."

Shea, who wasn't a toucher, put her hand on Annie's arm. "Whatever I can do to help, all you need is to ask."

Annie wanted to hug her, but just nodded and led the way outside, remembering in the nick of time to get the bag of equine medication. Despite the chance someone from her past had seen her on the internet, she felt lighter than she had in years.

"I INVITED HIM TO COME LIVE here," Irene said, just before she sipped her bourbon and sweet tea.

Tucker put down his fork. "What did he say?"

She sighed. "No."

He wasn't surprised. "He's got a life in New York. Friends."

"But we're family." Irene's voice had gone rough, which wasn't unusual however much he wished she could accept the situation.

"Christian needs time, Mom. It hasn't been long since he found out his father refused to let you see him. Most of his life he thought you didn't want him."

"You stopped being angry ages ago, and Rory Andrews stayed away from you out of spite."

"I had Dad. And you. I was lucky. Christian only had Rory and whatever stories he made up." Funny how Tucker never thought of Rory as being related, much less his biological father. His hazy memory of the man didn't even seem real, more like a fictional character in a story Tucker had read as a kid.

"You know I wanted to keep both of you." She took another drink, and this time it wasn't a mere sip. Soon she'd ask him for a refill, and he'd give her one. The drinking wasn't a problem, though it could head that way if she wasn't careful.

But how could he blame her? Tucker's own guilt weighed on him, and he'd been a child during the divorce. Was that the reason his desire to find Leanna Warner had become a borderline obsession? Why he'd been tempted to go early, to hell with his commitments?

No, he had to play it smart. He'd already baited the hook by suggesting the possibility of a large donation to Safe Haven. He'd put time between the email he sent and the day he was to arrive. She wouldn't be suspicious because no one looking for her would give her that much time to run. She'd accept that he was exactly who he claimed to be—a rep for a benevolent foundation.

All he had to do was be patient, observant and ready to take her down.

WELL PAST MIDNIGHT, TUCKER stretched his neck before he looked again at the papers he'd spread over the desk in his bedroom. Every one of them related to Leanna Warner, and every one of them intrigued him in a way that was keeping him awake despite his exhaustion.

She didn't quite add up. Her parents had been and continued to be social climbers. Joseph Warner was an attorney who'd worked for one of the most prestigious firms in New York, but he'd never made partner. His wife was an assistant manager at a design firm, again, second tier, but living among the elite.

According to Christian, Leanna had fit in so well with the wealthy young Manhattan scions and entrepreneurs that he'd been shocked to find out that she was a fundraiser. When he'd looked closer, though, he'd seen that her "designer" clothes and accessories were clever knockoffs. It was her personality and flair that let her get past all the normal barriers.

Christian would know about that kind of thing because he was in the same boat. His finance degree had gotten him only so far in a city that thrived on connections, but his audacity had helped make him a hell of an investment manager. No wonder the two of them had decided to team up. They each wanted a lifestyle that was just out of reach.

Reading the background material was helpful, but he had to check his bias at the door. If he let his emotions take the reins there was a risk he'd miss something important, or jump to conclusions. But there was no denying that Leanna was extremely clever.

On paper, she seemed the least likely person in the world to have stolen money. But if she'd had nothing to do with the fraud, why disappear? The logical conclusion was that she'd wanted to let Christian take the fall—except she hadn't tied him to any real evidence. One transaction record, even an email referring to an offshore bank account, could have put Christian squarely in the bull's-eye. Instead, Leanna had been forced into a life of hiding and his brother had just enough of a stain on his reputation to cripple his future.

Though she'd made off with over $500,000, she'd left each charity's seed money in the account, which, he suspected, was a clever way to avoid notice. At least until the whistle was blown, and then things had happened quickly. She probably hadn't had time to clean out the rest of the funds. But who could be sure of her reasoning?

So many discrepancies and oddities made it difficult to figure out her end game. Good thing Tucker was a patient man. He wouldn't make the mistake of acting rashly. If she had something that would nail her, he'd find it. Then turn her over to the D.A. gift-wrapped all nice and pretty.

He turned off the computer and gathered his materials. Most of what he had were printouts, but there were also several articles from New York newspapers, two yearbooks, four different brochures that Leanna had created and a short stack of photographs. The alarm was going to ring in under six hours, and his agenda was full all the way through Sunday. He wished he wasn't committed to the Rangers game, but it was more business than pleasure, so no choice there. It had been a long time since he'd been to a game for the fun of it.

He stripped down to his boxers and climbed between the sheets. As tired as he was, he should have been out like a light, but images of Leanna…Annie…kept spinning on a loop that wouldn't quit.

3

ANNIE LOVED THIS TIME OF YEAR. She breathed in the cool spring air and squinted at the Rockies still wearing their lacy snowcaps. Safe Haven didn't have many cows or calves to monitor. Even if they had she wouldn't have minded the job of running stock. Working out here in the big north field under the open sky seemed more like therapy than a chore.

She heard the pounding of hooves and forced herself to calmly turn in her saddle. Of course it was Will Woodruff riding out to take her place and not guys wearing suits and badges coming to slap handcuffs on her. Twenty-four hours had passed since Shea had deleted the photo, long enough to assume that if the wrong person had seen it, Annie would've been picked up by now. But not long enough to stop her from jumping at every shadow.

That didn't mean she'd let down her guard, but…she had to stop dwelling on it. The odds were in her favor and she'd decided to take the risk. In the meantime, she had a hell of a lot of animals and people counting on her.

"Afternoon, Annie. Anything I should know?" Will, who'd been a wild man in his heyday, a cowboy renowned for breaking the meanest horses and taming beautiful women, was in his sixties now and a valuable volunteer.

"Everything's fine. Anything exciting back at the ranch?" she couldn't help asking.

He looked at her as if she were nuts. "Not a thing."

They chatted for a minute, then she took off for home base, ready for some lunch before she moved on to chores in the barn.

Her first task after washing up and getting coffee was checking her email. A message from the Rocking B ranch made her pause. After reading the long email three times, she still pinched herself, just to make sure she was conscious. Then she went to the Texas ranch's website.

Looking at the list of grants and gifts the philanthropic arm of the Rocking B had shelled out through the years made her break into goose bumps. Those people didn't mess around. When they gave a worthy nonprofit funding, they gave enough to matter.

With shaking fingers, Annie bookmarked everything, then got out her cell phone. Good thing Shea picked up or Annie surely would've burst.

TUCKER LOVED TO FLY, AND EVERY time he went up in the Cessna, he thought about his father. It had been Michael Brennan's idea to send Tucker to flight school. The old man had been progressive in his thinking, and the ranch showed it.

The CJ2+ had earned its keep, despite the hefty price tag. It seemed as if Tucker's attention was always needed yesterday and flying gave him the freedom to respond immediately. It would be good to have the plane nearby when he met Annie Sheridan. There was always a chance that she'd want to give herself up. He wasn't counting on it.

The email exchange hadn't been as illuminating as he'd

hoped. Although he found it interesting that Shea Monroe was so invested in the workings of Safe Haven that she'd authored most of the correspondence.

A quick search of Monroe's name had prompted Tucker to send a link to George. He confirmed that she had high security clearance and was connected to some government programs that could be worth a fortune if sold to the right party. Tucker found it hard to believe that Leanna Warner would go to a backwater town like Blackfoot Falls without a good reason.

He shook his head, knowing he'd passed the point of no return given all he'd invested in that one vague online photo. Although the fact that the picture had disappeared without a trace, even in the computer's cache, was suspicious in itself. Fortunately, he'd saved it to his hard drive.

Annie's emails had focused on logistics, informing him of the airfield in Kalispell, the nearest moderately sized town that had accommodations and car rentals. He'd booked a room at the Hilton Garden Inn, reserved an SUV.

The closer he got to Montana, the more he thought about meeting the woman who had taken over a large portion of his brain. She confused him. Intrigued him. While he'd done his fair share of tricky negotiations with savvy competitors, he had the feeling his skills would be tested to the limit.

He'd have to be on his toes. Remember what lurked behind the beautiful face. And not for a second forget what she'd done to Christian.

ANNIE LOOKED UP FROM THE TABLE where she'd stacked copies of the Safe Haven board meeting agenda. Time had decided to slow down to a snail's pace, giving her a wonderful opportunity to let worry overshadow every bit of potential good that might come from Tucker Brennan's visit.

Safe Haven was too small. There were only a handful of permanent part-time volunteers. Because of their remote location, even if she could attract more help, they had to be local, and she'd already dried that well.

No, the problem was, most every animal sanctuary she'd researched had a visitor's program and a welcoming atmosphere for potential adopters. She couldn't even try to have guests because there wasn't a hotel in Blackfoot Falls.

She'd hated telling Brennan he'd have to fly all the way from Dallas, then drive to Safe Haven. And she sure hoped he'd like the food at Marge's, because that was his only choice. She just wished he would get here already.

No; in fact, what she really wished was that he would stop by, hand her a huge check, then go. Although she'd researched his credentials down to his alma mater, strangers made her nervous. Brennan lived miles away from her old stomping grounds in Manhattan, but there was always a chance that he knew someone who knew someone....

God, she had to stop thinking like that. Instead, she collated, stapled, put paper into file folders. In the end, it ate up ten minutes. Ten. And Brennan wasn't due for another hour or so. She'd never survive.

She could change, but no, she'd wait. The clothes she had on—work jeans, old tee, boots—were perfectly fine for day-to-day. It didn't matter that she smelled like a barn. But she would prefer to spiff up a little for the big shot with a checkbook. Nothing too fancy, just better jeans and a clean shirt.

Talk about a different life. In the beginning, she'd missed shopping like crazy, but she'd adapted. Learned to cook a little. She'd have killed for a pricy latte...okay, still would. But there were advantages to living on this very thin wire. She'd also learned to sew, and was grateful for the training because she'd had to patch up more than a few animals. Safe Haven survived due to the kindness of a few key players, like the vet, Dr. Yardley, who donated what time he could. Mr. Jorgensen from the feed and hardware floated loans for grain and other supplies. In fact, the whole sanctuary was built out of goodwill and patience, but Mr. Brennan could change all that.

Thanks to Shea, Annie had seen the difference an infusion of cash could bring to a two-bit operation like Safe Haven. But she remained cautious. Hope was only a friend in small measure. She didn't dare put herself in a position where she might fall into another pit of despair. It had taken her almost a year to climb out of the last one.

A quick knock at the door was followed instantly by one of the school kids ducking his head in. "Pinocchio's gotten stuck in the fence by the water pump."

All thoughts of Tucker Brennan vanished as Annie grabbed her gloves, followed the boy out of the cabin and ran as fast as she could.

THE DRIVE WAS PLEASANT, considering the circumstances. Tucker had only been to Montana for business, and never this far north. Looking out at the Rockies and the acres of lush land brought back memories of his early days when he'd still been learning about ranching from the ground up.

His father had made sure he'd done every job the Rocking B had for a cowboy. It had been hard work, but worth as much as his college years. His apprenticeship had given him more than just hands-on experience; it had given him perspective.

He barely noticed the town of Blackfoot Falls from the highway. It was like a thousand others across the country with a local diner that served great home-cooked meals, a bar that offered cheap beer, pool tables and country music.

All he cared about was that it was thirty miles from the Safe Haven turnoff.

Finally, he saw the big wooden sign that marked the entrance to the sanctuary. He was early, hoping the surprise would give him a slight edge. He liked to take stock of people when they were flustered. They revealed more than they knew.

So he slowed the rented SUV to keep the dust down as he headed for the main buildings. He passed one pasture with a half dozen horses, none of whom were particularly bothered by his vehicle. They looked pretty decent for rescue animals.

The fencing was sturdy, if old-school, about what he'd expected. According to the info he'd gathered on Safe Haven, there had been a few corrals, a barn, two stables and a cabin standing when Annie took over. Clearly, she'd made improvements.

His pulse revved as he neared the buildings. In one glance, he'd know the truth. But the truth alone wouldn't be enough. He'd have to use every moment he could to catch her vulnerable and get the evidence he needed. Even if it took a couple of days.

He pulled into a small parking area. There were several trucks lined up, mostly pickups, a tractor that had seen better days and a short yellow school bus.

Behind it was the cabin that had to be Annie's living quarters. She hadn't been kidding when she said it was small. But the working buildings gave a good first impression. Well spaced, old, but taken care of. In back of the barn he saw a small crowd of folks standing in a semicircle, as if they were watching a fight. Something pretty fierce, if the dust coming from the center was any indication.

He jumped out of the SUV, his inner alarm bells ringing. As he approached the crowd, he saw that the onlookers were kids—high school age—and two adults, a middle-aged woman pressing a hand to her throat and a petite twenty-something holding the arm of one of the teenagers, preventing the boy from moving forward. They all looked worried.

And then he heard it. The cry of a panicked, bleating goat.

He jogged the last few feet until he could muscle past the outer ring of spectators. It was a pygmy goat whose horns were tangled up in some high-tensile wire. Despite the name, pygmies weren't that much smaller than other breeds of goats, and the situation was dangerous. The woman trying to free him was taking a hell of a risk. Goats were notorious for their fear response. They kicked and struggled so fiercely they sometimes died from their hearts giving out.

Tucker knew the best thing to do was let the goat be and hope he tired himself out in time for intervention. Because a person trying to save one could well end up needing a doctor.

The woman making that mistake was Annie Sheridan. He had to admit she made quick work of cutting free the wire, but he could see she'd been battered and bruised. Her blond hair was damp with sweat, her face smeared with mud and blood.

The kid next to Tucker was a big beefy guy whipping the side of his leg with a pair of thick gloves.

He nudged the boy, who did a double take. "Lend me your gloves."

"Annie told us not to step in," he said. "It could be dangerous."

"I understand."

The boy looked him up and down, then handed him the pair. Tucker slid them on as he shouldered his way closer to Annie and the struggling goat.

She had just managed to cut the second to last wire curled around the goat's right horn when the back-leg kicking started again. Tucker ducked what could have been a very unfortunately placed hoof, then lunged forward, one hand on the back of the animal, the other grabbing on to his horn.

"What the... Get out of here, you idiot!"

"Cut the damn wire." Tucker was holding the goat's head back, just enough to unbalance him so he couldn't lean on his front legs. "Now."

Annie, grunting as the goat's body slammed her in the side, got the final wire cut.

Tucker had to use both hands to steady the terrified creature, while Annie quickly and efficiently cleared away the loosened wire fragments from his other horn.

The goat was free now, but he didn't know it, and Tucker didn't want to release him until Annie was out of the way. But she was too busy shouting at him to move to see that his position was stronger.

It was someone from the crowd that finally got her attention. An older man ran up, yelling, "Annie, get the hell out of there."

She did. Quick on her feet even with that prodigious frown on her face.

Tucker stopped looking at her and focused on making his own exit. It took a highly uncoordinated jump straight back, after which he nearly fell on his ass, but the goat did the right thing and ran toward the barn.

"What the hell were you thinking?"

For the first time, he got a good, clear look at the woman who'd just yelled at him, her fury uncompromised by her dirty face or her breathless exhaustion.

He didn't answer. He was too busy accepting the fact that he had found Leanna Warner.

4

"WELL, THIS IS PERFECT," Annie said, shaking her head. "Of course you're Tucker Brennan."

"And you're Annie Sheridan."

She nodded, made an abortive move to shake his hand, but her gloves were still on and her body had decided to alert her to a whole symphony of hurts and burns. What she would feel like when the adrenaline faded was going to be torture. "Welcome to Safe Haven," she said. "You're bleeding."

He followed her gaze down to his arm where there was now a rip in his shirt. There was blood, but while the cut was long, it wasn't deep. "Damn. I like this shirt."

"Sorry about that." She looked him over, just beginning to appreciate that the man in front of her was in a league she didn't come across anymore. The McAllister brothers were prime examples of tall, dark and handsome, no doubt about it. The sheriff and Matt Gunderson, too. But Brennan had a different kind of good looks.

Even with the rip in his shirt and those hefty gloves, she could picture him sipping champagne at a ritzy social event as naturally as riding the range. He wasn't New York fancy, though, which became very clear when he tugged off the gloves. There were some calluses, and he had a tan that wasn't perfect enough to have come from relaxing at the spa.

He was a gentleman rancher, certainly...with thick dark hair, a strong face and intense green eyes, all of which she shouldn't be noticing. He was doing his own inventory of her assets and liabilities, and she couldn't begrudge him. Though if he'd been another man she might've found his close scrutiny a bit creepy.

"Let's head to the cabin," she said. "I can patch you up there."

"I'll be fine. You, on the other hand, are a mess."

"Um, yes." She couldn't help but smile as she glanced down at herself. "Yes, I am." It could've been worse had she already changed to her good clothes. She looked over her shoulder toward the barn. God bless them, the kids had already returned to their chores. Although they'd be leaving soon. "Actually, I need to make sure Levi is tending to Pinocchio before I do anything else. We can get you a cloth to put on that cut, if you think it can wait."

"Yeah, this is nothing." He waved dismissively. "I'm assuming Pinocchio is the unlucky goat."

She nodded, leading him across the mix of packed dirt and gravel that became a muddy pit during rainy season. "He's a curious guy, and he never seems deterred by the messes he gets himself into."

"Goats can be difficult."

"Every animal in Safe Haven can be difficult. I think they sign some kind of agreement before coming here." She gestured vaguely. "Prelude to the tour. This is where we house the goats and chickens. We have twenty-two goats as of yesterday. We're always on the hunt for new families for them, but only for milking and breeding, not for meat."

On a shelf by the door, she picked up and folded a clean

rag from a pile and handed it to him. He pressed it against the cut, hissing a little.

Annie figured he would be fine for the next ten minutes or so. He was a rancher, so he understood that her first responsibility was to the stock. "The chickens, they kind of came with the place. Sometimes I'll wake up to new hens, more so roosters that people have dropped off."

She watched Tucker scope out the barn. Feed was safely stored behind big fences. The coops were spacious and well maintained. The goats had new water tanks from a central well, which had been the most expensive improvement since she'd taken over. No more lugging pails. Cleaning troughs? That job would never disappear. But then, that was something the high school kids helped with.

"That must be Levi," Tucker said, looking toward a bale of hay where the older man sat petting Pinocchio gently as his wife, Kathy, worked on cleaning the goat's wounds.

As Annie slowed her step, Tucker did, as well. No need to spook Pinocchio any further. Not that the other animals paid that any mind. Chickens wandered and pecked, making a racket that had become white noise to Annie. Some of the other goats were nursing or filching scratch from the hens. There were stalls for resting and birthing, and stacked bales of hay for the baby goats—kids—to find their legs.

"It's a great setup," Tucker said.

"We're always at capacity." Looking on, she sighed. "That's what's hard. So many in need, and we try not to overcrowd the barn. I've tapped out the locals for the most part. Though we're lucky to have an animal rescue pilot living nearby. Jesse has taken special cases to better-equipped shelters."

"How's Pinocchio doing?" Tucker asked, speaking to Levi and his wife.

"Banged up some," Kathy said, "but he'll be fine once

he gets his calm back. He's a devil, this one. If he wasn't so darn adorable we'd have pitched him out ages ago."

Both Levi and Annie laughed. "The day you pitch out an animal is the day we close up shop," Annie said. "You're worse than all of us."

Kathy's kids had left the nest. She and Levi, a former teacher, had been married for thirty-two years. She'd grown up in cattle country, and her wiry body was fit and strong. At sixty, she could still lift a fifty-pound bag of feed without breaking a sweat.

Her husband was just as sturdy. He didn't let his arthritis stop him. "What the dickens were you thinking, jumping into that mess?" he asked, frowning up at Tucker.

The slow curve of his mouth and amusement in his eyes said he wasn't normally spoken to in that manner. "I saw an opening. I took it."

"Could have got yourself killed." Levi shifted his stink eye to Annie. "And you sure as hell know better. Just who do you think would take over for you if you got hurt bad? You need to think of that before you rush in next time. We can't save everyone," he said, his gaze softening as he turned back to Pinocchio. "Much as we'd like to."

Annie wanted to change the subject quickly. The last thing she needed was for Tucker to think she was irresponsible. She couldn't very well yell at Levi for speaking the truth, but did he have to be so blunt with Brennan standing right there? Grasping for the quickest exit she could think of, she winced, touched her side and breathed a soft, "Ow."

TUCKER'S ATTENTION FLEW TO Annie. Her face didn't show the pain she had to be feeling. But she could be hiding something serious beneath those well-worn clothes. "We should get you fixed up," he said.

She nodded, and all he could think of was that seeing

her pictures and even the videos had not prepared him for this striking woman. He'd known she was tall, but in heels she would just about reach his height of six-one. Even with the grime smeared across her cheeks, he could see she had smooth, creamy skin. Her lack of concern for her appearance finally struck him. She'd given him a rag but hadn't taken one for herself.

Once she wiped off the mud, he wondered if her eyes would still look so blue under those thick lashes. And her hair was…interesting. He'd bet she cut it herself, but it somehow made her look more appealing. Her beauty was a perfect cover, all right. Of course Christian would have been captivated by her. Hell, any man would have.

She cast a final look at Pinocchio, then turned for the door. Tucker paced himself so he could get a look at her from the back. Long and lean, she walked with utter confidence. Another puzzle to work out. Why? Why had she run, only to end up working her ass off out in the middle of nowhere?

He got a quick look at the stable as they passed by. The younger woman he'd seen earlier approached Annie with a smile. "You okay?" the woman asked.

"Fine. Banged up a bit. But fine." Annie turned briefly to Tucker. "This is Melanie Knowles. She teaches at the local high school and is responsible for bringing the kids you've seen out here. Mel, this is Tucker Brennan."

He shook the woman's hand, but she was clearly too concerned about Annie to bother with him.

"You need some help?" she asked, nodding at the already blooming bruise forming on Annie's forearm.

"I'll be fine. All the help I need is that you and the gang are here."

"We've got you covered," Melanie said, then nodded

at him and circled back to the stable, where more of her charges were waiting.

Annie had developed a slight limp as they finally made their way into the cabin. He reached to hold the door at the same time she did. The awkward dance ended with her the victor. Then she nearly ran into him when he stepped inside and stopped dead still.

This was more like a line shack than a cabin. A crappy line shack at that. There was a beaten-up table in the center of the small room, three mismatched chairs pushed under it. A counter held a microwave while a toaster oven and a big coffeepot flanked the sink. On the sideboard sat a computer, and above that was a large chalk duty roster that listed volunteers, chores, memos and reminders. Under the sideboard was a dorm fridge. A leather recliner had been pushed so far up against a wall he doubted there was any chance of it actually reclining.

Stairs led up to a loft, which he imagined was her bedroom. The only other door had to be the bathroom, and that was it. He could probably fit the entire place into his walk-in closet at the ranch.

She touched his arm to sneak around him, making him jump. "Sorry. The bathroom's back there. Why don't you go in first and wash up? You should probably take off that shirt and let me have a go at that cut."

Tucker nodded and made his way to the bathroom, maneuvering around the table. He noticed a brass lamp, the only decorative object on the lower floor. There were no pictures, no trinkets, no nothing. He assumed the cupboards were as sparse as everything else. It would have made a perfect home for a monk. But hard for someone who had things to hide. With no space to spare, she'd have to get creative.

He'd sure like to get a look upstairs. If there was anything tying Leanna to her past, she'd keep it close when she was most vulnerable.

The bathroom was so small it made his jaw drop. The toilet desperately needed replacing, and next to that was a very tiny shower. There was enough room to turn around. That was it. The plastic curtain was too long for the bar, and he couldn't picture any woman he'd ever known who would last two days in this miniature house.

The pedestal sink looked old with its stains, but clean. Underneath, there was a medical kit, and above, a wooden cabinet with a small mirror.

His hand hit the shower enclosure as he took his shirt off. Putting it on the closed toilet, he soaped up. He checked his torso for bruises and cuts, but there was only one on his upper right hip, and while it was getting ugly, he'd survive. The cut on his arm stung, and it started bleeding a little, but it was shallow and would stop soon. No stitches needed, although an aspirin would be welcome.

Using one of the fresh-smelling towels, he dried off, grabbed his shirt and the medical kit and went back to the main room. "It's all yours," he said.

Annie opened her mouth but didn't speak. Instead, she stared at his bared chest. He knew he wasn't anything like one of those six-pack guys in catalogs, but he kept himself in good shape. The way she blushed surprised him, but then again, this was ostensibly a business meeting.

"I made some coffee," she said, finally, and that's when the aroma hit. "You'll find everything you need, unless you want cream. I do have some goat milk in there, though."

"Thanks."

He watched her go, feeling huge and clumsy in this small room, although he normally wasn't. But as he investigated, finding mugs along with plates and glasses and utensils, he realized how organized Annie had to be to make things work.

What was the use of running away with the money if this is how she had to live? There weren't two mugs that matched, or two plates. Everything looked secondhand. The fridge had very little to say for itself—the milk, a couple of bags of greens, some condiments, two beers way in the back. A tiny freezer section held a couple of frozen burritos and ice trays.

It wasn't surprising that the most abundant food in the cabin were packages of ramen noodles. This was worse than a dorm room.

She came out of the bathroom with her T-shirt untucked. She'd lost the pink on her cheeks, but she wasn't back to meeting his gaze. "Please sit," she said, kicking out one of the chairs.

"Can we have coffee while we do this?"

"Yes." Her demeanor changed with that one word, her face somehow expressing real pleasure without having to smile. "Of course."

So, without the smudges on her smooth cheeks, her eyes were still that incredible blue. He liked her mouth, as well. Full lips, well-defined and naturally pink. She wore no makeup, and she sure didn't need any.

He tensed when he realized what he was doing. Twenty minutes since he'd met her and he was already getting distracted by her looks. Christ.

She blinked, then lowered her lashes. "Go ahead," she said, with a jerky tilt of her head that had him cursing himself for staring too long. "I'll get the supplies sorted, then fix myself a cup."

Together, they made it through the dance of moving with only one open path. She almost avoided his chest, but that one brush of her shoulder made them both freeze as if they'd done something illegal. Annie cleared her throat, and he managed to ignore the contact.

He sat down with his coffee and tore open a package of gauze while he waited for her to fill her mug. The situation was perfect for his purposes. Sudden intimacy with a relative stranger was something no one could plan for. He would find out more about Annie in the next ten minutes than he would being shown around the sanctuary. But only if he stopped allowing himself to be distracted. She was a stunner, no argument there. Knowing how she'd used her looks to dupe his brother made him more the fool if he fell victim.

Along with her coffee, she brought a wet cloth and clean towel to the table with her. A pair of scissors, antiseptic and other first-aid needs had already been laid out. He watched her eye his arm, her top teeth toying with her bottom lip. She winced a second before she swabbed him with alcohol, and so did Tucker.

Far from the cool distance of someone used to causing pain, her expression was the picture of concern. A sharp inhale through clenched teeth, a soft, "Sorry," as she used a second swab. Once she covered the cut with gauze, her shoulders relaxed, and she was again the confident woman in charge. What he couldn't tell yet was if her empathetic response was completely false.

"Thanks," he said. "Now you."

"Oh. No. I can handle it."

"I doubt it," he said, watching her reluctance turn into another blush. "I was there."

When she finally responded it was with a weary sigh. "Okay, but I know it's nothing." She slowly got to her feet, looking as if she'd rather be walking barefoot on hot coals. "It's my back. I got caught on a wire."

He turned in his seat as she stood directly in front of

him, his eyes level with her leather belt. Now that he was looking for it, he could see spots of blood on her shirt. She lifted it carefully, exposing a long stretch of what would have been perfectly pale skin. Instead, there were two sizable bruises that were coloring in darkly.

"I don't know," he said, in no way faking his own concern, which made him uncomfortable. "Maybe you should get these checked out. It looks bad." He touched the worst of it with careful fingers.

Annie inhaled sharply. "If you'd stop poking at it."

"I'm trying to make sure there's no internal hemorrhaging."

"I'm fine. I've had worse."

"This one's over your kidney. It could be dangerous."

"I know there's no real damage," she said, lifting the shirt higher, but now with evident tension running through her. "I know because I was kicked by a horse years ago. So, the cut?"

"Right," he murmured, the word coming out low and slow as her bra strap came into view. It was the least fancy bra imaginable. White, no frills. A sensible bra that had no business looking like that against her pale flesh. Just as he had no business noticing.

The bruises hurt him to see, and the cut was no picnic, but it was impossible not to notice the rest of her body. The sleek elegance of her lines, the curve of her waist, the indention of her delicate spine. This close, her scent came through. Yeah, she was no rose petal, not from a foot or so away, but from inches, she smelled like a ripe peach. Damn his senses for the traitors they were. He murmured another curse.

"What? Is it that bad?"

He cleared his throat and moved his gaze to where she'd been bleeding. Now that he had some focus, he saw it wasn't a bad cut, on par with his own, but there was no way she could have taken care of it herself.

Tucker got a swab at the same time he pulled himself together. "No. It's fine. But it's gonna sting like hell."

"Go for it."

He did, and this time, their roles were neatly reversed. He winced—especially with the feeling so present in his memory—although he didn't apologize or make any noise at all. His job was to be efficient. Observant. He had a rare opportunity in front of him, and he was so busy thinking with his dick it was slipping away.

"This was some introduction, huh?" Her laugh was high and nervous. "I'm really sorry—"

"Do not apologize. I completely understand." Good. Back to business. "I saw a quarter horse that looked ready to foal. How many mares are pregnant?"

She seemed to relax even though he was taking the second swab to her cut. "We've had two births so far, both healthy. Besides Glory, one more is close enough to get her own birthing stall, and another one is showing. That's it, because we're keeping the mares separate, but they're the last of a large herd that was kind of dumped on us. Most of them were taken to a horse sanctuary in Wyoming, but we've got the rest.

"Thankfully, they're pretty healthy now. Some—" She stopped when his fingers touched her skin as he worked to adjust the gauze before taping it. "Some of them were undernourished," she continued. "And the vet was here a lot in the beginning. We've got a line on new homes for a couple of the stallions, which is amazing. It's going to be hard to place them."

"I'll take a look at them, if you like. I can't promise anything, but I know some people who might be interested, and they're not too far away."

"Yeah, distance is a problem for us. I'd appreciate any help you can give."

"Okay," he said. "You're all set. Are you sure there's nowhere else you might need help? I can get Melody in here, if that's more comfortable."

"Melanie." Annie dropped her shirt. "And no, but thank you. If you're up for it, we can take a real tour. You can bring your coffee with you, or we could finish it here if you'd rather." She gave him a quick smile, then handed him his shirt.

He stood, slipped it on and angled away to tuck it in. When he faced her again, she was drinking her coffee, her gaze focused on something other than him.

Was she thinking of another life? Of future plans? She understood that the Rocking B Foundation gave sizable grants and gifts. It could turn this little operation into something to be reckoned with, and considering they had access to aircraft, the potential for animal services was huge. Or maybe she was just thinking about how the foundation money, along with the stolen investments, could build her a dream home right across the border in Canada.

"We can walk and talk," he said. "That is, if you're not too sore. But I'd like to grab another cup of coffee."

"There's no such thing as too sore working a ranch. I guess you already know that."

Not the way she did. He'd been part of a big machine. Yes, he'd had to learn all the grunt work jobs, then those that took skill. But very few times had he faced the cold of a winter morning alone, when every animal in sight was counting on him for food and shelter and care.

There was nothing simple about sanctuaries. He'd investigated a hell of a lot of them. Each time, there was one individual or couple who were the lifeblood and soul of the operation. Those who gave up any sense of a normal life to the welfare of the animals.

She'd been doing it almost on her own for two years. He didn't have the faintest idea why. Penance made no sense. Not when she could go back to New York and really make things right. How was it he hadn't anticipated her working like a dog? What had she done with the money she'd already stolen?

"You know, I've got to make a couple of phone calls." He checked his watch, then made sure he looked at her when he added, "Would it be okay if I met you in the stable in about twenty minutes?"

There. A flash of panic that was gone in the blink of an eye. Just long enough for him to see her gaze fly to the loft and back. She didn't want him here alone. Not for anything. But he simply waited her out.

"Sure. No problem. I'll see you there."

"Thanks. I won't be long."

Annie picked up her coffee mug, then set it in the sink without taking another sip. She hesitated at the door as if she was working out what to say to him, but in the end, she stepped outside. He watched her walk down the path, his phone to his ear.

The minute she was out of sight, he headed straight up the steps. His heart was beating too quickly, but there was nothing he could do about it. He wasn't used to subterfuge. He'd always believed in facing his problems head-on. But this case was the exception to all his rules.

He saved the obvious for last, moving quickly around the room, looking at the floorboards, the wall for any possible nook where she could have something stashed.

With no paintings and no closet, there wasn't much territory to explore, but he took his time. The dresser was filled with clothes, packed tight. Still, he pulled each one all the way out to look underneath the drawer. Nothing.

The bed was intact, as far as he could tell without stripping it completely, but underneath...

Coffee cans. Four of them. And an old-fashioned suitcase. That's what he opened first, checking his watch, appalled at how long everything was taking. She could come back any second, and she'd have every reason to call the cops on him.

The suitcase was full of paperback books and music CDs. He checked every pocket twice, flipped through the books and popped open the CD cases, but he didn't find anything noteworthy. Disappointed, he shoved the case back under the bed.

He hit one of the cans of coffee, and just to be sure, he checked. It was unopened coffee. So was the next, and the next.

The fourth one had an unsealed envelope. Inside, it was a single sheet of paper with a typed number and password. He was certain the number was for a bank account. There was also a driver's license in the name of Alison Bishop, with a picture that sort of looked like Annie, and a roll of cash thicker than his fist.

After he took a picture of the license and the account number, he put it all back under the bed just the way he'd found it. Then he got the hell out of there before she caught him red-handed.

5

THE KIDS WERE GONE, AND WITH them, Melanie. It was relatively quiet outside, as quiet as it ever got around Safe Haven. Annie was grateful because she had to calm herself before she went in to see the pregnant mares. They didn't need her fear and worry, and no one would ever convince her that animals didn't respond to human energy, good and bad.

It made perfect sense that Brennan would need to make some business calls, that he'd like to be alone when he made them, and also not have to worry about the background noises that were inescapable on the property.

She'd already decided that the website photo had not blown her cover. She'd researched Brennan and he was legit. Even Shea had done some of her magic and given him the thumbs-up.

Besides, a man like Brennan wasn't the type to go snooping. And even if he did, he wasn't going to look inside coffee cans stored under her bed, for God's sake.

Some deep breathing made her wince, but it also helped calm her down long enough to dismiss her concerns about him discovering her real identity. Which left her wide-open to worry about everything that had actually gone wrong since he'd arrived.

Annie had known for a while now that wishes and daydreams were a waste of time. That didn't stop her from wishing that she could start the day over, or at the very least ask Tucker to leave and come back tomorrow.

She didn't even dare think that nothing else could go wrong because that was just inviting catastrophe. She still had on her stinky, now bloodstained and torn work clothes. The man she so desperately wanted to impress had walked in on her making a fundamental mistake in caring for animals—one that could have cost them both physically, and certainly may have cost her financially. What foundation wanted to invest in a sentimental idiot?

Then, to make everything a billion times worse, the libido she'd managed to stifle for two long years had decided to rejoin the party by filling her mind and body with so many hormones she could barely see straight. She'd actually had to bite back a moan when he'd touched her.

Thank God he'd put his shirt back on. It didn't erase the memory of his muscled chest and the smattering of dark hair, or his small hard nipples or the perfect V from his broad shoulders to his trim waist. But at least she didn't have to dig her fingernails into her palm to stop from touching him back.

Dammit, now she wished she'd brought her coffee. And taken some ibuprofen. She thought about going back to the cabin, but they kept a bottle of aspirin in the stable med kit. She should have offered him something when she'd bandaged him, but with all that chest showing, she'd been distracted.

"Is everything okay?" Tucker asked from behind her. "Are you feeling dizzy?"

She must have jumped a foot. She hadn't heard him walk

across the gravel. He had to think she was nuts, standing in the middle of the path, staring at nothing. "No, I'm fine. Sorry, just thinking about... We should go check on the horses."

"Right." He smiled, although it seemed a little forced and made her edgy. "FYI, in my younger days, I spent a lot of time in foaling stalls."

"Good, then you can help if it looks like things have progressed that far. I think Glory might foal tonight. She's been up and down a lot today, sweating like crazy. I wouldn't be surprised if her water's already broken."

"Is this her first?"

Annie shrugged, but she was relieved that the conversation was squarely in safe territory now. She could talk animals till the cows came home and feel fairly sure she wouldn't make a misstep. "Don't know. She arrived pregnant and undernourished. We fattened her up, but it's impossible to say what that period of malnutrition did to the fetus. So Doc Yardley is on call, and I'll be setting up camp out here tonight."

"You've done this a lot, then?"

"Often enough to know when to call for help." She stopped at the stable door. "I've been meaning to ask," she said, looking directly at him as the sun cooperated and moved from behind a cloud. The butterflies she'd never expected to feel again came back, but she couldn't afford not to watch him, because the issue had been bothering her since that first email. "You're the head honcho of the Rocking B ranch. Your foundation has a director by the name of Rafael Santiago. So how come you're here instead of him?"

Oddly, the question made him smile. A half grin, actually, the right side of his mouth lifting for a few seconds. "I think it's important to do some things personally."

"You go to each nonprofit yourself?"

"Not all of them, no. This is a special case."

That made her blink. "Why?"

"Okay, I admit it." Tucker gave the impression of shrugging without moving his shoulders. "I may have had some other business in the area, but I figured this might be a nice break from the daily grind."

Annie laughed. "You picked a lousy place to find rest and relaxation, Mr. Brennan. I only have six permanent part-time volunteers. Levi and Kathy have been keeping an eye on the mares today, but they leave when the sun sets. I'm pretty much it until eight tomorrow morning, and I'll have my hands full. I can't even offer you dinner, unless you want a frozen bean and cheese burrito."

The half grin came back. "Hey, at least I got to wrestle a goat."

This time her laugh was accompanied by a sense of ease. "To each his own," she said, although she didn't for a minute think his answer was silly. Her last real vacation had been spent working at a horse rescue shelter in upstate New York.

"Come on," she said. "This is the primary stable, used for horses who need special attention. We've got plans in the works for a separate quarantine stable, but we don't have the funds yet. The economy hasn't helped us with a lot of donations. Although our board chair, Shea Monroe, has been doing wonders in that area. We've got several email campaigns running with more planned."

"It's Tucker," he said.

She blinked, stopped walking.

"Not Mr. Brennan."

"Oh, right." Annie walked him into the stable proper, making sure to move slowly, talk softly. "The stalls are twelve by twelve. That wall serves as the barrier to the half of the stable we use to house the newcomers. There are four stalls back there. The four in the middle are for those who are hurt, and we keep the nearest four for foaling. They're really too close to the doors but we don't have much choice."

Annie let him take his time looking around the big white structure. Considering it was almost twenty years old, the stable was in good shape. The man who'd originally built Safe Haven had come from Idaho, and he'd worked his tail off to save whatever horses he could.

Tucker walked past the pregnant mares to check out the other horses that were in sick bay. None of them were contagious, just needing special attention.

Levi and Kathy were inside the empty foaling stall next to Glory's. "Hey," Kathy said, keeping her voice low and calm.

"How's she doing?" Annie asked, taking a look at the mommy-to-be. Glory was a sturdy black quarter horse with a blazing white star on her forelock. She was lying down on her nest of fresh straw but her agitation was clear.

"She's fine," Kathy said. "We've got a bet going on what time her water'll break. I say ten."

"I think it's gonna be midnight," Levi said. "You gonna call Doc Yardley?"

"He's supposed to come by later, but everything's going okay. I can handle it."

"You know," Kathy said, "we can stay."

"No need." It was Tucker's voice coming from behind her, and Annie jumped, even though he'd kept the words soft. "I'll stick around."

"You don't have to do that," Annie said. "I can manage, and you just flew in today. Wrestling goats is exhausting."

His grin made her want to flip her hair back like a teen at the mall.

"I'd like to stay," he said. "We used to tell all our most embarrassing stories waiting for the foals. It was fun."

Annie turned to face him, wincing as she tried to cross her arms over her chest. If she'd had a brain, she would have iced some of the worst bruises before heading out to show off the sanctuary. She really needed to get that aspirin. "We've got a ton to go over tomorrow, including that ride across the property you asked for in your email. Besides, I don't recall telling embarrassing stories being an essential part of foaling."

His casual wink made her pulse leap. "You just haven't been to the right stables."

Kathy and Levi both laughed, but that got Glory struggling to her feet, so all attention went to her. As soon as she was standing, Annie entered the stall to comfort her. She moved slowly, holding up her hands and whispering the same soft nonsense she had since Glory had been brought in. She'd made a point of touching the mare a lot, letting the horse become familiar with her scent and her hands.

The foal was moving and there was no sign of excessive distress. With luck, there would be little to do but observe and clean up after the birth. As she left the stall, everything was quiet except for the familiar sounds of horses. Snorts and breathing, shifting straw, a soft nicker from Cocoa, who was waiting her turn to go into labor.

She walked to the open stable doors, knowing Tucker, Kathy and Levi would follow. As soon as they were far enough away to speak normally, Annie said, "You guys don't have to stick around. It's almost six."

Kathy looked from Annie to Tucker, then back again. "You're awfully stiff. Did you put something on your bruises?"

"I'm fine, Kathy. Thanks."

"I brought you that liniment for a reason," Kathy said.

"You've got us here for a bit. Go fix yourself up, and stop being a stubborn mule. You might be up all night, for heaven's sake."

Annie wanted to shoo her friends on their way, but Kathy was right. The ointment would help. "All right." She turned to Tucker. "Other than that cut, are you aching anywhere? Kathy makes up her own salve, which works wonders."

"Nope, I'm fine. But I'll watch out for Glory if you two want to get home."

Kathy didn't even respond to Tucker. Instead, she hustled Annie back to the path toward the cabin, which meant that she wanted to speak to Tucker without Annie hearing.

Resigned to her fate, Annie gave in to the ache in her hip as she headed for the jar of salve. It didn't help that it was so easy to picture someone else applying the ointment, someone who looked mighty fine without a shirt on.

TUCKER COULD HAVE USED something to ease the minor aches that had cropped up in the past hour, but he was more interested in paying attention to the couple who were about to give him a heartfelt testimonial. He hadn't gotten this far in business without being able to read people. In fact, that particular skill had been a primary factor in keeping the Rocking B strong through the recession and the drought.

Sure enough, Kathy, who looked tired but determined after the eventful day, approached him the moment she could. "Here's the part that isn't obvious, Mr. Brennan."

That stalled Tucker's arrogant assumptions in their tracks. An excellent reminder that he wasn't the only one who could read people.

"That girl," Kathy said, pointing in the direction Annie had disappeared, "has gone without basics so she could feed the horses. Not that she'd ever say a word. We didn't know in the beginning. But things started to add up. So some of us decided to bring treats, meals, coffee, because she won't take a penny for herself. Not a penny. Everything goes to the sanctuary."

Glory was making some real noise, so they moved inside. Levi turned on the bank of red lights, bathing the space in an eerie kind of beauty, which allowed them to observe but wouldn't disturb the mare. Her water hadn't broken, but she was nesting again, rearranging the straw as she prepared for the birth.

"She hardly ever comes to town," Levi said, his arms crossed over his broad chest, staring at the horse, not Tucker. "When she does, it's to get supplies or to find help in one form or another. Not for her, mind you, but for the animals."

"Any idea why?" Tucker asked.

"Why she gives so much, you mean?"

He nodded at Kathy.

"She doesn't talk about herself. We don't even know where she's from, really. She just showed up one day, volunteered. It wasn't two weeks later that Edgar, the man who built Safe Haven, went back to Idaho to be near his grandkids."

"Thanks for letting me know." Tucker gave her a nod. "But I'll warn you, as I've warned Annie. I can't make any promises. I have a board of directors myself, and I have strict criteria that has to be met before we can offer funding or grants."

"Oh, we know that," Levi said. "But we couldn't let you leave without telling you that you'll never spend a wiser dollar. It's not just the animals who benefit. You should see how much the high school kids are learning. Everyone who comes to volunteer at Annie's sanctuary is the better for it."

"I believe you," Tucker said. He had no reason not to.

For whatever reason, Annie had decided to play her role to the hilt. She clearly needed these people to be on her side. Just like Christian had been so enthusiastic about her before the money went missing.

Now that he'd found that account number, Tucker was even more certain that whatever Safe Haven was, it was also a cover for Leanna. Or a stepping stone to something bigger. He had some theories about the account number and the license in the coffee can. It had to be an exit strategy, but why hadn't she used it yet? Was access to the stolen money contingent on some future date? Was someone else holding the key? Another kind of partner, perhaps?

He needed to find time tonight to send the pictures to George, get him working on making connections, putting the pieces together. In the meantime, he had to keep his wits about him and look beyond his physical attraction. He'd run across some smooth operators before, but Annie was in her own league. She confused him. He couldn't nail down her motives or predict her next move. He felt as if he was missing one vital piece of information that would unravel all the mysteries.

Levi and Kathy shook his hand and made sure he knew where the birthing kit was. He watched them meet Annie halfway to their truck. Huh. He'd expected Kathy to touch Annie. A hug maybe, or at least a friendly hand on her shoulder. But they kept to their own personal spaces, and said their goodbyes with nods.

When Annie returned to the stable, the first thing she did was hand him a couple of pills and a bottle of water. "Ibuprofen."

"Thanks."

With a nod, she went to check on Glory, but from outside her stall. Tucker followed until he was close enough to smell a hint of liniment, which he didn't mind at all. He supposed it had a lot to do with his own history. The scents of a ranch were home to him, including the one that overshadowed the sweet peaches that lay beneath....

At the thought a bolt a lust shot through him, making him reel. It was crazy. Maybe he was too tired to be sticking around when everyone else was gone. He'd like to think he was made of stronger stuff, but his reactions were off. Just to get some distance, he went to check on the other pregnant mare.

The two empty birthing stalls still had shavings instead of pure straw. He walked deeper into the stable, really looking at the other horses. A sturdy-looking mustang had a bandage over one eye. Then there was a buckskin Appaloosa who seemed unaffected by the human comings and goings, but had some bandages on her flank. She reminded Tucker of a horse he'd ridden for five years, a great palomino who'd been so good-looking, no woman for miles could resist her.

"You can't see it from here, but Pretty Girl was quite a mess when she arrived," Annie said, indicating the Appaloosa. She'd come close, and Tucker kept his gaze on the mare. "She'd tangled with some barbed wire, and it took a lot to patch her up."

"You do it well."

"Nothing like on-the-job training. I put another pot of coffee on while I was at the cabin. I'm going to make us a couple of thermoses. How do you like yours?"

"Black is fine. If you tell me where things are, I could do that for you."

"That's okay. I think we have a wait. I'll be back in plenty of time." Annie started walking, but stopped before she stepped outside. "You promise you've done this before?"

"I swear." He put his hand up, and she sighed.

When she had rounded the path out of his sight, he let himself breathe again as he got out his cell to speed-dial George. Tucker updated him on the attached photographs, what he'd found under the bed, and then asked him to look for evidence that Annie might have been working with someone else. Maybe someone who was pulling her strings.

"You think she was coerced?" George asked, not sounding as surprised as Tucker might've expected.

"I don't know. I'm trying to look at every angle. Some things don't make sense about her. I'd rather we kept an open mind. If she's not the only one behind the embezzlement, I want to know. You find anything else since we talked?"

"No. That account number might just be the answer we're looking for."

"It might," Tucker said. "I'll call you when I can."

After he put his cell away, he found a couple of blankets in the area they used for supplies, and brought them up front. If they were going to wait, they might as well get comfortable. Besides, it was better to be as discreet as possible when mares were foaling. They could spook so easily.

He spread out the blankets against the wall in the stall next to Glory's, then went back to the supply area to gather everything they'd need for the arrival of Glory's foal. He couldn't see well with the red lights, but it didn't matter because the packaging told him most of what he needed to know.

The same could not be said about Annie. If he'd returned to his hotel room, he would've gone straight to his computer. Hell, he wouldn't have been able to wait that long. He had an iPad in his briefcase in the rental, and he'd have stopped way before Kalispell to reread every word in his files. Watch the videos, look at the pictures as if he didn't have each detail seared into his memory.

Thing was, he'd only been with Annie a few hours, so maybe him not being able to figure everything out wasn't all that strange. On the other hand, now was the time to turn every stone, including the ones that seemed least likely.

He thought about his mother spending Tuesday evening on her own. He'd asked if she'd made other plans, but he'd anticipated her answer. She would end up in her room, eating off a tray. She'd watch TV, mostly reruns of shows she'd liked when his father had been alive.

Tucker had heard her talk to him from time to time. As if he were in the next chair. Irene was lonely. What scared him was his suspicion that she wanted all the forgiveness she could get from Christian because she didn't plan on sticking around.

He rubbed his tired eyes, then stared at his watch until it came into focus. Annie was taking a long time. A whole lot longer than making a pot of coffee required. Maybe she was checking her hiding spots, making sure he hadn't been snooping. Great. He'd probably disturbed something that made her suspicious. For all he knew she'd grabbed her coffee can and run.

As if on cue he heard the rumble of an engine. He jumped to his feet, half expecting to see her taking off in that old green pickup, leaving a cloud of dust behind. As soon as he made it outside, he saw that it was a truck, a late-model four-door from what he could tell, coming down the road toward Safe Haven. He'd assumed they'd be alone for the rest of the night, but maybe the local vet was arriving to check on the mares.

Annie came around the edge of the path, stopping to stare at the oncoming vehicle. Tucker couldn't see her face, but her body stiffened and she brought the thermoses she carried up to her chest.

A moment later, she relaxed again. The truck was familiar to her. The vet, or perhaps a friend. Although Kathy and Levi had suggested that Annie didn't have many of those.

She shot him a look, and when he nodded, she changed course for the parking area. The big truck had settled next to the old green pickup. He watched four people climb out. Two men, two women. The men were both tall, one dark haired, the other light brown, both dressed as his own hands would be, but that didn't mean a thing in cattle country. He knew professors and CEOs who wore Stetsons and jeans on a daily basis. The smaller woman was a brunette, the other a redhead, also wearing jeans. Annie was taller than both of them.

Instead of continuing to stare like a tourist, he went back into the stable. Glory was on her side, huffing, uncomfortable, more obviously stressed. He watched for a bit, but he couldn't see enough from this angle to tell if there was cause for concern. She settled, though, so Tucker went to the birthing kit and checked it out, even though he knew exactly what he'd find. Subdued voices approached, and he walked outside. One guy held a cooler, and the other had a big picnic basket. A good distance from the doors, Annie and the two women waited. The closer he got, the more uncomfortable she appeared.

"Kathy called Shea, so they came with dinner and help if we need it. Doc Yardley is stuck on a call at another ranch, most likely for the night," Annie murmured, sweeping a glance from the newcomers to him. "This is Tucker Brennan."

"Shea Monroe," the brunette said, and held out a stiff hand, which he shook.

"Ah, yes, the chairman of the board," he said. "Pleasure."

Annie nodded at the guy holding the drinks. His hair

was shorter than his cohort, almost a military cut. "Jesse McAllister."

"The pilot. That's a great service you run," Tucker said.

"It's a co-op. I just fly where I'm told."

"And this is his sister, Rachel."

They greeted each other with smiles.

"I'm Matt Gunderson," the other guy said. "Hope we're not intruding, but according to Shea, you two are in for a long night."

"You're not intruding." Annie's words sounded sincere, but she wasn't looking at any of her friends, and the thermoses were back in place against her chest.

"Have we met?" Tucker asked, staring at Gunderson.

"Don't think so."

"Wait, you're a bull rider. I've seen you ride in Dallas. You won the nationals in Vegas last year."

Matt nodded. "That'd be me. Listen, I know you guys have to keep it down, make sure the mares are doing okay. We can just drop this stuff off and be on our way, unless you think you'll need a hand."

Annie looked up at that, first at Matt, then at Tucker. He couldn't read her expression, but if he had to guess, he'd have said she'd tell them to go. But then she looked at Shea, and her shoulders dropped. "No, stay. In fact, you guys can tell Tucker about town, and the new boardinghouse and stuff. I have to go check on Glory." Annie shoved one of the thermoses at him, then walked into the stable.

The surprise wasn't that he'd guessed wrong about her telling her friends to leave, but at the deep sense of disappointment he felt at Annie pawning him off. He tried to convince himself that his frustration was because of his investigation, but he knew that wasn't quite true.

6

ANNIE HAD KNOWN THAT LETTING people into her solitary life was going to be trouble. She just hadn't guessed the form it would take. She'd tried to make it clear that any generosity or kindness flowing her way should be directed solely at Safe Haven. People being nice to *her* made her want to scream.

It wasn't their fault. They had no idea who she was, what she'd done to her parents, to the people her stupidity had harmed. Even with what Shea knew, she probably still didn't get it. They all saw this person saving animals and figured she must be a wonderful soul, selfless to the core.

The only reason she hadn't chased them away was because of Tucker. Annie should have been prepared with some food and drinks. Despite all appearances, she hadn't been raised in a barn.

But at least she could trust Shea with Tucker. Unlike Kathy and Levi, Shea was more concerned with getting financing from Tucker's foundation than talking up Annie. As if she hadn't figured out their little ploy.

Glory was really sweating. She was on her feet and moving around, and as Annie watched, the mare's placenta ruptured. Annie wouldn't leave again until the foal dropped. Glory went down again in the middle of her nest.

Annie held her breath as the first signs appeared. Thank God it was two front hooves and muzzle. Still, a lot could go wrong.

"She looks good."

Annie exhaled, starting at Tucker's voice so close to her. She had to stop doing that. She hadn't heard him or sensed him enter the stable, let alone come right up to stand by her shoulder.

She didn't reply, her focus entirely on the mare. The contractions made her wince, but the baby was coming on fast. Before it seemed possible, the foal was mostly expelled, but Mom needed a few minutes to gather more strength before the next push. When it came, there was a beautiful soaking mess of a foal, and everything from that moment on went like clockwork.

Tucker never interfered at all, but he was right there when Annie took care of the umbilical stump and handed her towels to rub the foal.

She had no idea what time it was when Glory set about bonding with her baby, except that humans were no longer welcome in the stable.

After a quick look at the other two mares and getting cleaned up at the deep, old-fashioned sink, Annie led the way out. She expected that everyone had eaten, or at least to find the picnic basket and cooler waiting for them, sans company. But that was clearly too much to hope for.

Matt opened the cooler and pulled out two beers. "Cause to celebrate?"

Tucker took them both and handed one to Annie. "Textbook," he said.

"Great. Let's eat." Shea headed to the parking lot, where

Annie saw they'd set up the food tailgate-style, complete with folding chairs.

Annie had to admit she was hungry. It had been an utterly nerve-racking day, and while her adrenaline was flowing now, she knew a crash was inevitable. Thankfully, it wasn't that late. Tucker could go home right after a quick bite, and she could at least try to get some sleep.

She had the feeling that no matter her degree of exhaustion, turning off thoughts of Tucker wouldn't be easy. So many things to process, not the least of which was the fact that every time he came within spitting distance, the flutters started up with a vengeance.

There were enough chairs for everyone, and whoever had set them up did her a favor by putting them in a large circle. The cooler was brought to the open tailgate of the pickup, alongside the basket.

"We've got sandwiches," Rachel said. "Roast beef, tuna and veggie on sub roles. There's chips and carrot sticks—"

"And cupcakes," Jessie added. Annie doubted he meant to sound quite so excited.

"Cupcakes and beer?" Tucker shook his head. "You Montana folks are culinary daredevils."

Rachel snorted, but somehow made it ladylike. "We had a whole ten minutes to pull everything together because someone who should have reached out earlier didn't," she said, pinning Annie with a mock glare. "Oh, and there are cold sodas and bottles of water in the cooler."

Annie really liked Kathy, but she was going to strangle her. "Just how many meals were you planning on serving?" she asked. "It's late. You guys all have to go home so I can get some sleep."

"We didn't know that the horse was going to foal so early," Matt said. "And I heard there was more than one ready to go."

"We only have one other mare in the stalls, but there's no reason to think she's going into labor tonight."

Shea looked at her. "Would you prefer that we left?"

Annie knew Shea wasn't being sarcastic or touchy. "No, really. I just hate keeping you all out like this. Tucker flew in from Dallas this afternoon, remember?"

"Don't worry about me," he said. "I'll be fine. I confess, I could eat."

Annie touched his arm with her hand before walking over to the basket. "Thank you for your help today. It was unexpected."

He stared at where her hand had been, then met and held her gaze in the weird light cast by two lanterns. "It's been my pleasure. A very memorable day."

She had no idea what to say to that, and honestly couldn't tell if he was simply being polite or flirting. The flirting part was probably wishful thinking, which was nuts because what in the world was that going to get her? The two of them would never happen. No way in hell.

She swallowed hard. What she hated the most? The need was back, the desire to touch and be touched. And if anyone could satisfy that itch, it was a man like Tucker Brennan. She stepped back, away from temptation, and did everything in her power to not turn and run.

TUCKER GRABBED A RANDOM sandwich and bag of chips, way too aware of the woman beside him. He'd flirted with her. Hadn't meant to, especially in front of her friends. The blame went to the long day at least for now, but when he was alone again, he'd have to have a serious talk with himself about appropriate behavior.

As no one else was sitting, he went for the farthest chair, hoping Annie would sit opposite him. He wanted to watch her from a distance. He would've preferred to observe from outside the circle so he could concentrate on what was important instead of chasing his personal fascination with the enigmatic Annie. Instead, food was grabbed quickly and everyone sat, leaving Annie the chair to his left.

"How did you find out about Safe Haven?" Shea asked.

Halfway to a bite, Tucker paused, the question catching him off guard. He thought about asking her the same question. A woman with her security clearance and computer skills didn't fit in this cowboy world.

"My foundation manager," he said. "I'm not sure precisely where he ran across this particular sanctuary, but he does a very good job of finding worthy causes."

She nodded slowly. "Perhaps I can speak to him. I'd like to know how effective our online marketing is. It's difficult to choose where to spend money and energy when there's so little to spread around."

"I'll make sure to get you that information."

It turned out the sandwich was tuna, and it was good. He'd been so distracted he hadn't realized how long ago he'd eaten, and for a few minutes he did nothing else.

Annie was chowing down, too, and it should have been far less compelling to watch her hunched over her sandwich as if she were afraid someone would steal it. But she managed to make it look sexy in a way that was slowing him down as his pulse sped up.

Damn, but she was a beautiful woman. That was another conundrum. Beautiful women often seemed to use their looks to get what they wanted. It was difficult not to, when the world around them made it so easy. Beauty was a passkey to so much. Even as children, teachers treated cute kids differently, everyone did. He'd been a recipient of that kind of bias himself. And he knew for a fact Annie had successfully used her looks to deceive Christian.

Yet, here she was out in the middle of nowhere, surrounded by livestock when she could have hidden in a hundred easier ways. He couldn't imagine the number of men who would have been happy to hide her, to keep her safe.

When he looked down, he realized he'd not only finished his sandwich, but actually used his fingers to capture the last crumbs of his potato chips. After a swig of beer, he went back to the basket. "Anyone else want seconds?"

"I'll take another beer as long as you're up there." That was…Matt. The rodeo champ.

"You still riding the circuit?" Tucker asked, handing Matt his beer before heading back to his own folding chair.

Matt didn't answer straightaway. "Yeah," he said. "I've got things here in Blackfoot Falls that are taking precedence at the moment, but I'm still riding."

"You'd better be," Annie said. "We've been talking about having a charity rodeo for Safe Haven. Trouble is housing out-of-towners. There's an old boardinghouse that's going to be fixed up, but we'll probably have to hold the rodeo closer to Kalispell if we do it in the next year."

"It's not a bad drive." Tucker sat, consciously slowed himself down while unwrapping his next course. His hunger was easing, not gone.

"Too much beer drinking at rodeos to have people driving afterward," Annie said.

Having a conversation made observing her easy. Although the way he was getting caught up in the view was a problem. "True," he said. "But a rodeo is a good idea."

"From what I saw on your website, your ranch is riding out the drought well," Jesse said.

All Tucker's plans to keep Annie engaged, to keep himself separate from the group, vanished in a discussion about cattle and the weather, which then segued into ranching innovations. By the time the eating and drinking had come to its natural conclusion, he felt every hour he'd been awake, and every ache he'd earned from his goat wrestling.

None of them would let him help pack up the impromptu picnic, but he was allowed back into the stable to check out the newborn. Already standing on wobbly legs, the still-damp foal was a sight to see.

Next to him, Annie sighed softly as they stood in the neighboring stall, keeping as quiet as possible. She had to lean into him so he could hear, and the contact against his arm wasn't helping things. "We should go," she whispered. Her warm breath skimming the side of his neck sent a jolt of awareness straight to his groin.

He nodded, made his tread as light as possible on his way out, Annie walking alongside him. For some reason the others were still there, all standing near the pickup. His knee-jerk reaction was disappointment. Dammit. Wanting to be alone with her was fine, even wise if he wanted to get information, but not when it was personal.

"What's wrong?" Annie asked, as soon as they'd reached the others.

"That," Rachel said, nodding at Tucker.

Caught in the middle of a yawn, he snapped his mouth closed. "I'm fine."

"You might be right, but we don't want to take any chances. Safe Haven needs your money." Rachel grinned, but she wasn't lying. "Our place is close by. We have a spare room you can bunk in for the night. Then you can go back to the hotel first thing to change and whatever."

"I assure you, I've lived in isolated places my entire life, and I purposely had only one beer. I can drive."

Jesse shook his head. "You'll pass more deer, cattle and coyotes than cars on the way, but that's not the problem. You're tired from flying and driving. Why take the chance when we've got room?"

"Besides," Rachel said, "you should get a look at the Sundance before you leave. You'll be surprised."

"At?"

"All the beautiful women who are staying with us," Jesse said, and grunted when Shea elbowed him.

"Excuse me?" Tucker looked to Annie, who smiled, at least for a few seconds.

"They've turned it into a dude ranch," Annie said, and then he recalled the website where he'd seen her photo. She'd been at the Sundance ranch when it was taken.

"Wait a minute." Jesse was obviously annoyed. "That's not true. Our main concern is raising cattle."

Shea and Rachel exchanged glances, then stared at their feet to hide smiles. Clearly the dude ranch operation was a touchy issue, and as a cattleman himself, he understood. But that didn't concern him. What did interest him was the opportunity to find out more about Annie from these people. And Shea…perhaps he should know more about her.

"Sorry," Annie said. "It's a working spread, but the dude ranch part is helping to transform the area. More guests, more tourists, more cash flow. And more opportunities to spread the word about Safe Haven. It's all good."

Rachel laughed. "Trust Annie to squeeze in Safe Haven."

He didn't think about it for too long. He would have preferred having his things with him, but the chance to gather information, and frankly, to get to bed sooner, was too strong an incentive to say no. "All right. Thank you, I'll take you up on that."

"Thank God," Annie said, sincerity softening her voice. Her lips lifted in a tired but sweet smile. "I'd never have gotten to sleep if I was worrying about you driving all that way."

That he instantly thought of staying right where he was,

bunking down on the blanket in the empty stall, made him shake his head. He needed a good night's rest. Desperately.

IT WAS ONLY WITH TREMENDOUS will that Annie brushed her teeth before heading upstairs to bed. She'd watched as Tucker had followed Jesse's truck down the road to the Sundance, then she'd done a final check on the horses.

The short walk to the cabin had felt more like a mile, and she'd made herself prepare the morning's coffee before she hit the bathroom. Now she had to climb stairs, but then she'd be horizontal and nothing would come between her and sleep.

An hour later, she was seriously contemplating bashing her head against the wall because her brain would not stop.

At first, it had been okay thinking about Tucker and wondering yet again if he'd flirted with her. She'd debated taking care of her suddenly awakened body, which was something she hadn't done in so long, she wondered if she remembered how.

It was only after those thoughts that she was reminded why she'd stopped. Being in exile, being a fugitive, eliminated all possibility of having any kind of anything with any man. For an indeterminate period of time, up to and including forever.

It had taken her a solid six months of denial to get to the stage where she didn't think about sex anymore. No, okay, longer than that, but she hadn't caved since. Though she'd had close enough calls that she'd become very judicious with her reading material, and careful with her time around other people.

Some thought she was shy. No problem, shy worked, because most everyone kept their distance. At first, she'd thought the McAllister men were going to be a problem, but her fear was so great, it overwhelmed her sex drive by quite a bit.

She'd become celibate in every sense of the word, and then Tucker Brennan.

It wasn't fair. He was only going to be in town a couple of days. She'd never see him again, but if she kept thinking about him, remembering the touch on her bare back, the quickening of her pulse every time she saw him staring…

Bodies weren't meant to be turned off like empty refrigerators. She was only twenty-nine, but she knew without a doubt that somewhere inside her there was a clock ticking away. Exhaustion had always been her best defense, but here she was after a brutally tiring day, and he'd broken through over a year's worth of defenses with a few touches and a good smile.

Her life, her entire life, was dedicated elsewhere. She'd done her best to never think about what she'd left behind, what she was missing. She worked until her body couldn't take it anymore. Then she did it again.

Tonight was an object lesson. Letting herself get caught up in the real world would do her no good. Tucker Brennan was a potential check. Financing. That's all. She'd better drum that into her foolish mind, because there'd be hell to pay if she didn't.

The sad thing was that she'd have to pull back from Shea, as well. It had been an experiment, a test to see if she could open her life up a little.

The answer was a resounding no.

7

THE STRANGE ALARM JERKED Tucker out of sleep so hard he felt as if he had whiplash. And damn, he didn't even have a razor or a change of clothes with him. It seemed foolish to shower when he had to put on the same shirt to go to Kalispell before he could return to Safe Haven, but yesterday clung to him with the scent of straw and stubborn goat.

So he showered and dressed. He would have killed for a cup of coffee, but he wanted to check in with George first.

Luckily, the private investigator was already up despite the early hour.

"I don't have that much to report," George said. "I've started working on the account number, which isn't an easy thing to trace, my friend, but we'll get there. As far as the driver's license goes, the ID number doesn't match the name or address. So it's a fake, but from the picture it looks like a decent one. I don't know that it'll bring us much more information. I did send the photo you took to some people I know, but don't get your hopes up."

Tucker had figured as much and tried to tamp down his impatience. He was more interested in the possibility he'd raised yesterday. "What about the coercion angle? Any evidence she was pressured into taking the money?"

George hesitated long enough for Tucker to tense. "Nothing's changed," George said finally. "Not since I checked a year ago. Leanna had no known criminal associates or unsavory friends or family problems. If she took the money under duress, I haven't seen any evidence. Doesn't mean I won't be looking. We did have a different agenda back then, and I might have bypassed something crucial."

"All right." Tucker rubbed his eyes. "You have anything on the men in her life?"

"There were a few in college, nothing too serious. When she worked at Keystone as a fundraising assistant, she was with a man named Alex Phillips. They were a couple for three years. He moved to D.C. and is now a lobbyist for a New York telecom consortium. He's married and has a son. No arrests, no ties to any scandals."

"Okay," Tucker said. "And Shea Monroe?"

"That's still tough. She's worked on highly classified projects, and if I tug too hard on any of those strings we could be inviting more problems than we want. I did find out that she's still under contract for something big, but I have no idea what."

"Do what you can with that. And maybe start looking at Annie's family more closely. It could be one of them in trouble, I don't know."

"Look, Tucker…" Shit, George was using his fatherly voice. "We never thought we'd get this far, right? I mean, worse comes to worst, we let the authorities know, they come in, do their own digging. Running like that makes her look awfully guilty."

Tucker's breath caught at the cavalier words. "We already decided that finding her isn't enough to clear Christian. I need to dig more and understand what happened, before the D.A.'s office gets wind of this. My instincts are telling me we're missing a big piece. I'm not even going to mention anything to Christian, not until I know more. So, do your best, huh?"

"You know I will, Tucker."

"I appreciate it."

His next call would have to wait until after coffee, because Darren wouldn't be in yet. Irene wouldn't be awake, either. Though Tucker wasn't sure he wanted to speak to her at the moment, anyway. She still didn't know his trip out of town was a fact-finding mission to help Christian, and Tucker aimed to keep it that way for the time being.

Now, it was going to be coffee or death. Personally, he voted for coffee, and he knew the day was going to be a good one because the scent of a rich dark roast greeted him halfway down the big staircase.

He'd known he wasn't the first one up, but he had hoped that he'd recognize someone in the kitchen.

Instead, there were a lot of young women. Pretty young women at that. They were bustling about with an older Hispanic woman, making what looked like enough breakfast to feed an army.

"Well, hello there."

It seemed early for a greeting like that, especially coming from an attractive brunette whose jeans were so tight he wouldn't recommend she do much sitting. "Morning."

"Who are you, and when did you get in?"

Another stare, this from a woman with a spatula in one hand and a smile that reminded him of this year's Miss Texas posters. "Rachel didn't tell us there were any men coming to stay."

"That's because he's not here for a vacation." At Shea's no-nonsense voice, Tucker turned. She entered the kitchen frowning at the spatula girl. "Rachel asked me to tell you that you're all leaving for Glacier National Park in an hour, whether you've eaten or not."

Tucker could tell the other girls were intimidated by Shea. He doubted they had reason, although she'd been a big surprise. The woman who'd written emails about the financial viability of Safe Haven—who'd outlined their immediate plans for fundraising campaigns and upgrades to the facility—had come across as a smooth communicator, one who had the kind of social skills that went along with certain high levels of government contracts.

What he'd found instead wasn't so easy to classify. There was a bluntness about her that wasn't rude, just… raw. He wondered if she could be manipulated, say, by a woman in hiding waiting to make a last big score before darting over the Canadian border.

The bad thing was, the very traits that drew him to Annie were what made her role in the theft all the more believable. Hell, even knowing what he knew, Tucker had been drawn in and wanted to at least give her a chance.

"Morning, Tucker," Shea said. "Coffee?"

"Please."

"I assume I should put it in a to-go cup?"

"I have a few minutes." He smiled at her unguarded sigh. "I thought maybe we could talk."

With a resigned expression and a glance at the guests, she took out a large insulated mug, poured, then handed it to him. "Let's go into the other room."

He nodded and followed her past the dining area into a parlor with an expansive view of the Sundance and the snowcapped Rockies in the background. She leaned against a wooden post, which would have fooled him into thinking she was comfortable if he hadn't seen how she avoided his eyes.

"If you had any questions about Safe Haven, about the financials or the fundraising, I mean," she said, "I can probably help you. Because Annie's very private."

"Really?"

Shea toyed with her cup, slightly lifting one shoulder. "Most of us don't know much about Annie except for her work ethic and her commitment to saving every animal she can. The things that matter."

"She works extremely hard. I could see that yesterday."

"She's driven, you know?" Shea met his eyes, her caution fading. Perhaps acknowledging Annie's dedication had earned him an ally. "Or maybe she just prefers the company of animals. I get that. Mostly I do, too."

Tucker smiled at her candor. "There are days, a lot of them, when I'd have to agree."

"Well, as long as you know that she's worked miracles with virtually no assets. I can only imagine what she could do with proper funding."

"I assure you, I'll give Safe Haven every consideration. So far, I like what I've seen. Is there anything else you can tell me that would help sway the vote?"

She blinked, then narrowed her gaze. "Like what?"

So much for bringing her over to his team. "I don't know." He paused to think. "In your opinion, what's Safe Haven's biggest selling point?"

"Annie."

Exactly the answer he wanted. "Well, there's a problem with that," he said, letting his words settle, then studying Shea's worried frown. "We don't know if Annie will be here long. She could leave tomorrow and then who'd run Safe Haven?"

Shea relaxed. "Annie's not going anywhere."

"She might get homesick," he said, and Shea shook her head with a sadness she quickly masked. "Or find someone and get married. Have kids."

"No," Shea murmured quietly, her gaze downcast. "She won't."

He almost felt guilty for the pain he'd seen flash in her eyes. But he hadn't caused it, not directly. Annie had. He'd bet his Range Rover she'd confided in Shea. Maybe he'd just found Annie's Achilles' heel. Which was perfect because Shea was a lousy liar.

This was good news. So why did he feel like crap?

"Thanks for the coffee," he said, holding up the mug. "I'm going to gather my things and take off for my hotel. I want to be back at Safe Haven early. Please tell Rachel and the others I appreciate the hospitality."

"No problem." Shea finally looked at him with a small smile, and he didn't doubt she was glad he was leaving.

The ride to Kalispell was a straight shot, and soon enough he'd put on clean jeans and a fresh shirt, and was reading over his files as he went through a quick room service breakfast.

Now that he'd met Annie, the material he'd gathered had taken on new shades of meaning. From her days in high school to her equestrian victories on horses that belonged to other people, he could see so much of the woman he'd spent time with. The data on her family didn't suggest anything unsavory, but he still felt that was where George should focus. Because God knew, families could be tricky.

He finished reading every document in his extensive files, knowing he should have left already. But he needed to do this now, before he saw her again.

His gut was telling him there was something big missing in the picture of Leanna Warner and her disappearance. The idea that someone behind the scenes had forced her to run had taken hold in him, and he was ninety-nine percent certain he was reading that correctly.

All the things that made no sense about her—how hard she was working, why she kept herself distant and alone, even her failure to ensure Christian looked guilty to the feds—came together if she'd been coerced.

Annie Sheridan was hiding, all right, but not from justice. He'd wager a hell of a lot on that hunch. Christian had to know more. Maybe something he didn't even realize was important.

If he wasn't afraid Christian would tell their mother, he'd call Christian right away. But his brother was still too angry to be trusted. Or maybe that was Tucker. Lord knew he didn't blame Christian, but his brother was filled with a very old rage. Tucker wasn't stupid, he knew Christian had been playing Irene, using guilt to get money, then ignoring her until he needed more. But he'd chosen to stay out of it for his mother's sake.

Better to wait, to see what came of George's investigation.

Tucker put his iPad in his briefcase, along with an emergency set of clothes, just in case, and headed down to his rental. It wasn't right the way he was itching to see Annie again. But there didn't seem to be a damn thing he could do about it.

THE INSTANT ANNIE WOKE UP, she knew something was wrong. The light. There was light coming in from the window, and she'd set her alarm…had she set her alarm?

With a hammering heart she looked at the clock. Ten. Ten in the morning, and God, Glory and the new foal. The morning feed. She jumped out of bed and almost screamed as all the aches and pains from yesterday hit her like a sledgehammer. Wincing and cussing all the way through throwing clothes on, she barely looked at what she'd hauled out of the dresser. Limping downstairs, she washed up so fast she probably skipped half her face.

Forget coffee. She hurried to the stable, trying to get her

heart to slow down and her brain to speed up. She caught her hip on the edge of the door as she swung herself inside and it was a lucky thing because she would have fallen at the sight in front of her.

Tucker Brennan stood at the entry to Glory's stall, his head turned, his brow furrowed and a single finger over his lips. "Quiet, he's eating."

"He's…?"

"The little guy," Tucker whispered. "He's been having some trouble this morning, but he's finally latched on tight."

"How long have you been here?"

"About half an hour."

"The feed. I have to—"

"Levi and Kathy are out there somewhere, said to tell you not to worry. They've got you covered."

She'd known the couple would come today, but they typically didn't arrive until long after the early-morning rounds. "I overslept."

"So I gathered."

"I never do. This is literally the second time it's happened, and the first was because of a power outage, but then I bought a battery-run clock."

His smile was warmer than it should have been. They were strangers, maybe would-be business associates, and that smile was meant for a friend. Something they could never be. "It was a long day yesterday. Come on over here and take a look."

She crossed the short distance to the side of the stall and made sure she didn't stand too close to Tucker. Especially after she'd found her stride slowing as she ran an appraising gaze down the back of his body. He had on jeans and a blue Oxford shirt. Sharp, clean and sexy as hell, and she hadn't even bothered to brush her hair. Great. Bedhead was one of her better looks.

Then she saw the dark brown foal with his skinny, knobby legs splayed so he could get up under his mom. Glory was munching away, calm as you please. "Oh, that is a sight."

"There might be another one tonight," he said. "Cocoa's on her way."

"It's a factory in here," she said. "Something big must have happened eleven months ago to the day for two so close together."

"Statistical probability, but I know what you mean. We see groupings a lot. Pheromones, I imagine, in the herd."

She nodded, liking this. Just talking. It was easier when she wasn't looking at him. "I need to do my rounds, catch up with Levi and Kathy. You can come along if you like, or stay. After, I'm going in to make coffee. I hope you'll join me at the cabin."

"I'll come with you now," he said.

He didn't follow her into the other stalls as she checked on the rest of the brood, but he accompanied her to the barn, where the chickens ignored them but only because the goats wanted all the attention.

Pinocchio, it turned out, was doing fine, and deeply unconcerned about his battle scars. Kathy, who'd sadly lost her own land due to hard times, started out smiling at Annie, but that changed in a flash to something far harsher.

Kathy's hand went to her hip. "I hope you're hurting like Hades, young lady."

"Gee, thanks. Yes, I am."

Kathy's big hair barely moved as she nodded. "Serves you right for getting in that mess with Pinocchio. You should've let him work himself into a frenzy until he passed out. Then you could have cut him free, and not got yourself in trouble."

Oh, God. Annie knew everyone meant well but she did not want to hear the same thing for a month. "He also could have died."

The older woman sighed. "There are always risks. Pinocchio might've died, and that would have been sad, but if you got sidelined…"

"Point taken. I'll do better next time."

"Levi finally got that part in for the feed truck. Should be working by this afternoon."

Annie grinned at the news. "Fantastic."

"Now might be a good time for you and Mr.… Um, sorry, my short-term memory's shot, don't take it personal."

"It's Tucker," he supplied.

Kathy smiled. "You and Mr. Tucker should take a ride out. Show him the field."

Annie and Tucker exchanged glances and laughed.

"What?" Kathy frowned at them.

"Nothing, really." Annie cleared her throat. "Tucker is his first name." It was weird for her, sharing a private joke with someone. No, not someone…with him. "We will get a ride in, but first we have to go over the books." She squeezed Kathy's shoulder, then moved over to give one of the baby goats some attention. "When are you two planning on leaving?"

"Not until this afternoon. We worked it out with Will. You're covered tonight. For as late as you want. This meeting is important to all of us, so take the time you need."

"Thank you," Tucker said. "The attitude of the volunteers tells me a great deal about an organization."

"Well, sir, we're all simple folks from around Blackfoot Falls. We believe the sanctuary helps everyone. To my mind, a community should be judged by how it treats its most vulnerable creatures. We're doing what we know in our hearts is right."

"I agree," he said.

"And I need coffee. I'll see you when we're done inside." Annie started walking before Tucker could see her sappy grin.

HALFWAY TO THE CABIN, Tucker decided to change things up, take a chance. See what happened. "As long as you're covered here at Safe Haven, how about dinner tonight?"

Her inhale told him the suggestion had thrown her off balance. So did the pause in her step. She hadn't expected the invitation. For a moment there, she'd been frightened. He'd seen it, but only because he'd been paying close attention. So far, they'd kept things professional. Dinner could mean anything.

"I've been wondering what motivated you to take over the sanctuary. I don't know much about you, and it's always interesting to discover what leads someone to this kind of life. It's not an easy one. You have to want it badly to put up with all the obstacles. I thought we could talk about it over a meal."

The flash came again, only for a second, and more contained this time, but it was important that he push her. More than ever, he needed to get to the bottom of this mystery. If she had acted under duress, as he suspected, he had to know. Not that he was forgetting about Christian. His brother was still his priority, but if he could get to the truth, it would solve both their problems.

"You know what? Let's see how the day goes." She hurried the rest of the way to the cabin, held the door for him. "Why don't we have that coffee and go over the books? Then see where we are. I mean, you're going home tomorrow, so—"

"I've moved some appointments around. Thought I'd attend your first meeting tomorrow, meet the rest of the board."

She looked at him as if he'd slipped a rug out from under her feet. He supposed he had. Trouble was, instead of taking satisfaction in throwing her off kilter, it seemed he wanted to catch her before she fell.

8

THE HORSE ANNIE GAVE TUCKER TO ride had been named Ronald Weasley, by a committee of four from the high school. She assured him that at one time, the majority of the cast from the *Potter* series had been in residence, but that a lot of them, including Harry, had found homes.

She rode Candy Cane, who'd become something of a favorite among the staff. The names and explanations behind them had taken them past the first and second corrals. Annie was grateful for the distraction, knowing she couldn't put Tucker off for too much longer. After the ride was over, she planned to shower and change, sending him to town on his own. After all, it was foolish to take one vehicle when he'd be going back to Kalispell for the night. She'd meet him at Marge's.

She'd debated calling him with an excuse after he'd gone to the diner, but that seemed like a surefire way to kill any chance of getting foundation funds. A man like him was used to conducting business over dinner. In New York she'd done it more often than not. There was no reason for her to think he wanted to share a meal for any other reason. At least him driving ahead would give her time alone to figure out what to tell him.

When she'd first arrived in Blackfoot Falls, people were
curious about her and of course they'd had questions. But
she'd been vague and firm, and for nearly two years no
one had pressed her about her past. God bless cowboys.
Not that everyone didn't gossip about her—she knew they
did. But that was fine.

Tucker had caught her off guard, that's all. Sure, he had
money, but at heart he was a cowboy. She'd been ready
to tell him every last detail about Safe Haven and all her
plans. She wasn't comfortable telling him lies.

It was bad enough she'd donned Annie Sheridan like
a new skin. On the few occasions anyone asked, she said
she was from back east. True. When they asked her why
she wanted to run Safe Haven, she said she'd always had
an affinity for animals, horses in particular. Also true.
Then she changed the subject. That wasn't going to work
with Tucker.

"This is gorgeous country." Tucker rode in a way that
made her feel like a klutz. "I'd forgotten what a real spring
looks like."

She wasn't a klutz. In fact, she was a good rider. But
Tucker had been born to the cowboy life.

"The drought has hit everyone in Texas hard," he said,
his baritone laced with sadness. "It's a different landscape
from when I was a kid. It breaks my heart."

"I'll bet," she said. "This is all Safe Haven land, you
know. It doesn't belong to the state or the Bureau of Land
Management. That's good, because we need the space.
But we're not incorporated, and if there's a fire, unless it
threatens buildings or livestock, it's only going to be managed, not fought. So the more snow and rain we have, the
better it is for everyone. Thankfully, this far north, we still
get a lot of snow."

"You have trouble with predators?"

"Much as any ranch out here. We've lost our share, but that's the way of it. The price for free range. Most of the cattle are just passing through, though. We're not equipped to take care of many, but people are quicker to take cows."

"That's good. What about the horses?"

She found herself urging Candy Cane to move faster. "We get a lot of abandoned horses. Too many folks have lost their homes, lost their property, including their ability to care for their stock. Cows are typically bought, but horses… There's a lot of sentiment around horses, even if the old-timers want to deny it. Nobody likes to send a horse to slaughter. Unfortunately, those same people aren't able to find them new homes. I'm sure it's the same story on your end."

"Every rescue shelter we support has a different set of circumstances unique to their location." Tucker looked around at the distant prairie, spread as far as they could see. "There are plenty of lakes here. Shade trees. Underground water flow. A horse might find a decent chance."

She nodded. "Good thing we have that because there's never a time we're not at capacity. Not a week goes by we don't have to turn someone away."

"That won't change if you get funding."

"It'll happen less. That's something to hope for."

He seemed to study her with a different kind of interest. "Safe Haven is lucky to have you. Whatever happens from this trip, the work you've put into this place is something you can be proud of."

"Thank you." Annie rode ahead a bit, trying not to let him see her confusion over the oddly ominous compliment. Had he already eliminated Safe Haven as a worthy nonprofit? Then why bother to stay for the board meeting?

Maybe they weren't ready for a gift yet. She'd run across

that in her fundraising efforts, where an organization would hold back money until certain goals had been met.

That would be a blow, but only because she was letting herself hope too much. Nothing was ever guaranteed. Especially when things looked brightest.

They weren't far from the field she wanted Tucker to see. Putting aside her worries, she let the excitement of this amazing project spur her forward. Candy Cane caught her enthusiasm and Weasley trotted along. The perfect breeze lifted Annie's hair, taking her out of her myopic panic for the first time since he'd mentioned dinner.

The day couldn't have been better. Green leaves and buds and early flowers were everywhere she looked, the scent of spring vivid, the sky an astonishing blue. Realizing she'd let this pass her by for half an hour reminded her to grab what she could while she could.

When Tucker caught up to her, she truly saw him, not as the man who could solve her financial problems or the nosy stranger who asked too many questions. He wasn't smiling or anything so obvious, but he looked happy. As if he belonged in Montana, at least for this day.

It was the contrast that made it so clear to her. Yesterday, this morning, Tucker had walked with an air of gravitas about him. Even when he joked around or drank beer from the bottle, he made an impression. You wouldn't want to tangle with this guy. She had the feeling if he went after someone, they wouldn't know what hit them until the dust had long settled.

"What's this?" he said as they got closer to the five-acre experiment. "How tall is that fence?"

"Seven and half feet. It's not finished, though. But we'll need to keep the deer out, so we had to go high."

"What's it guarding?"

"The future," Annie said, her voice tight with anticipation of his reaction.

When he looked at her, sparks lit up all through her, but she decided they were a result of the project, not Tucker. "Show me."

"Well, the view's not impressive. Yet." She urged Candy Cane into a burst of speed and led Tucker around the fence to the western gate. Of course, he could see through the wires, see that there was nothing but flat ground, not even plowed yet. But she wanted him to get a feel for how big the plot was, how big the idea was, so she slowed, dropped from her saddle and waited until he'd done the same.

They walked beyond the gate. "This is going to be a field of alfalfa," she said. "Five acres. Before the tractor engine blew, we'd just started to amend the soil, so it won't be ready for planting until next year. There are some issues with irrigation that need to be handled before we can truly make this work, but I know we'll do it. All old school. No motors, no generators. Just wind to push the water through."

"Huh," he said, mostly to himself, turning his head as if trying to picture what this land would look like in five years. In ten.

"If it works, which it will, it'll be the first of many plots growing feed. Not only to make Safe Haven more self-sustaining, but to help future interns learn about alternative agricultural methods. We want to train ranchers to be able to take care of their land using creativity to build and grow.

"This fence has been a large-scale project guided by the high school kids. They did all the fundraising and recruited the help they needed to get the fencing equipment. They're still working on it, and maybe it'll take more than a year, but I don't think so. We've discussed making it a cooperative, so that other ranches might be able to start rebuilding. But that's pretty far in the future."

When he turned to her this time, his smile made her blush. There was no doubt that Tucker was impressed. More than she'd hoped. "This is remarkable. Really outstanding. It was your idea?"

"I'd mentioned it as a faraway dream, but Melanie and the students, they ran with it. She's so committed to using the sanctuary as an educational resource that great ideas are all stacked up, just waiting to come to life. She's amazing."

"She isn't the only one."

Annie's cheeks burned. She ducked her head and tucked her hair behind her ear. When she looked up again, though, something had changed. The smile had frozen on his face, and his gaze seemed troubled. A second later, the grin lifted, and if she hadn't looked up at the right time, she would have missed it entirely. "Is something wrong?"

"Not at all," he said. "I'm very glad you brought me out here." He moved closer, and for a moment she thought he was going to touch her arm, but then he ended up running his hand through his hair. "You have any more surprises up your sleeve?"

"Nope. This was it."

He nodded. "Maybe we should head back, then. I've got some phone calls I need to make, and I know you have things to do. We'll figure out dinner arrangements on the way."

"Sure, no problem." Annie mounted her horse, unsettled and disappointed. The moment had been so perfect. What had changed? She couldn't think of anything she'd done wrong, but then, she wasn't always quick to see beyond her own enthusiasm. So much for her ace in the hole.

MARGE'S DINER WAS…A DINER. It wasn't crowded. Only two men sat at the counter sipping from white mugs. Tucker nodded to them as he passed on his way to a booth in the back. A waitress appeared, poured the men refills, then brought him a menu along with a curious smile.

Strangers had to be infrequent guests in Blackfoot Falls. The interstate was an hour away, and the town was small. And, except for the Sundance, didn't seem much like a tourist attraction.

He'd arrived early, but he didn't mind waiting. He was still worrying over a moment of clarity he'd had when Annie had shown him the five acres. She'd swept him away, as thoroughly as if she'd been a magician. Standing there, he could see her vision of the future, her commitment to changing her slice of the world for the better. For one powerful moment, he'd been ready to take out his checkbook.

And then it had hit like an unexpected tackle. She wasn't Annie Sheridan. He had no idea who she really was. Except that she had to be one of the best fundraisers he'd ever encountered. He didn't give his money away, not without a lot of forethought and reason, but she could have taken him for a completely different kind of ride.

He didn't doubt his intuition. He believed that there was far more to the story of Leanna's skipping town than Christian had said, because she wasn't the greedy, unscrupulous woman he'd described. Tucker had more faith in himself than to think his judgment was so far off. But that didn't change the fact that he didn't *know*. She could still be under someone's thumb, still need money to get herself out of a desperate situation. Although that was a stretch. Running an animal sanctuary was the worst way he could think of to raise a lot of cash. And her enthusiasm for the place… she hadn't been faking that.

He raised his gaze just as she walked through the front door.

She'd changed into a different pair of jeans, a fresh shirt. He couldn't help wishing she'd worn a dress, something more sophisticated that would have shown off her tall, lean body, the way she carried herself. She must have amazing legs.

He stood as she approached the table, then sat when she slid into her side of the booth.

"You're early," she said.

"I've only been here a few minutes. It's a nice place."

She grinned as she looked at the row of uniform booths along the window facing Main Street and the old-fashioned counter with black vinyl and metal stools. "It's the only place."

"There are more restaurants in Kalispell. We could go right now."

She picked up the menu, shaking her head. "Cocoa might foal tonight, so I can't even be here for long."

He picked up his menu, too, noticing straight off that they had a homemade beef stew featured. "You know, you never did answer my question about how you ended up in northern Montana."

She studied him, her lips pressed together and her eyes grave. "Serendipity. I'd heard about Safe Haven when I was traveling. I've always been into horses, and animal sanctuaries were a passion. When I came to Blackfoot Falls, I never intended to take over Safe Haven. That just sort of happened."

"Traveling from…?"

"Back east." She studied the menu, then smiled up at him. "I haven't eaten here much, but I do know about the popular dishes. The chicken fried steak is homemade, battered right here, and the burgers are supposed to be off the charts. Oh, and if you like crispy fries, Marge's is the place."

Instead of calling her on her subtle misdirection, Tucker found himself caught in her gaze. He leaned forward, aching to break down the walls that she'd built so well. There were no obvious lies in anything she'd said. She hadn't blinked or given any tells that he could see. It only made her more of an enigma.

God, but she was beautiful. His hand moved across the table until he almost touched her. It was a near-miss, stopping himself just before contact. There was too much he wanted from this woman to let his attraction subvert his plans.

Unfortunately, what he saw reflected in her eyes wasn't the hint of fear he'd been expecting, but a want he understood too well.

Her lips, pink and lush and unpainted, parted, revealing her white top teeth. If she were his, he would kiss her for hours, make them both crazy for more. But he wouldn't give in. Not until she was quivering in his arms.

Then again, maybe he'd do that as an encore. He doubted he'd have any self-discipline with her.

"You two need a minute?"

The intrusion made him almost knock his water glass over. Quick reflexes from the waitress saved the day, but the accident gave him time to regain his composure.

When he glanced across the table, Annie was looking anywhere but at him.

"Yes, another minute would be good," he said, checking the waitress's name tag. "You don't serve alcohol here, do you?"

"Nope," Karen said. "You'd need to go to Sadie's down

the street for drinks. But we've got great milk shakes. Our ice cream is awesome. Though you might wanna save that for dessert, because we've got fresh huckleberry pie just out of the oven."

Tucker sniffed the air. He could smell the pie. "I might just skip dinner altogether."

The young woman laughed. "Don't do that." She leaned in a little. "I'd go for the stew tonight. Or the rib eye. Can't go wrong with either one."

"Thanks, Karen."

Tucker was almost afraid to meet Annie's gaze again. Afraid of getting drawn in. He didn't seem to have many defenses against her. The ones he'd brought with him were toppling like dominoes with every new look.

Annie put away her menu, then folded her hands on the table, gripping them tightly. She looked at him, but only in quick snatches. "I did a lot of work around stables when I was young. Never owned a horse. Wanted to. My family thought it was a passing phase, something girls go through until boys come along. Not for me."

"None of the boys were more interesting than riding?"

"Not what I meant." She smiled. "I was a perfectly normal girl, went on dates, even had a couple of relationships, but my passion for animals, and horses in particular, never dimmed."

"Did you plan on running a sanctuary?"

"I wanted animals in my life. Somehow. And see? I got what I wanted. I may not have the life I'd imagined, but I'm where I need to be. Doing things that matter. I'm better here, in northern Montana. I'm the right person in the right place."

"Yes," he said. "I've met a number of people who have given up a lot to run animal rescues, and you're one of the most dedicated I've ever met. But—and you can tell me to mind my own business—don't you get lonely? It doesn't seem like you have many opportunities to meet new people."

"I'm not lonely at all," she said, sitting up straighter. Her jaw flexed a bit, then she exhaled and relaxed. "Alone doesn't automatically mean lonely, you know."

"I do."

"So what about you?"

"Hmm?"

"Are you married?"

"No." He laughed.

Her face lit with amusement. "Why'd you say it like that?"

"Like what?"

"Like it was an absurd notion. You don't care for the idea?"

"I think it's a fine institution. And when or if I meet the right person, I'll consider it."

Annie's left eyebrow quirked up. "Who would fit that bill, Tucker Brennan? A Dallas socialite, perhaps? Someone with a high-class education and Texas roots?"

"Really? That's who you think I am? That I'd be more attracted to a pedigree than a person?"

Her shoulders dropped a little, as did her head. "No. I was being a smart-ass. Pardon me. I don't know you, but from what I've seen, and what I know about how you ranch and your priorities, I'd say you'd want someone you could trust and respect. Someone you could admire."

"Don't we all?" he asked, the conversation hitting him hard for some unknown reason.

She smiled at him, and it was about the saddest thing he'd ever seen. "I think I'm going to try that stew. And take home a slice of pie."

He nodded, accepting the segue into safer territory.

But for the rest of the meal, the conversation felt strained. They laughed too quickly at things that weren't that funny. Pretended the sporadic silences were comfortable. Stole glances, ate quickly, tiptoed.

After he'd paid the check he realized he couldn't have said what the food tasted like. At the door he asked, "You parked on the street?"

Annie shook her head. "Behind the diner."

He touched the back of her elbow. It hadn't been a planned move, and once the connection had been made they both froze for a second. But he didn't drop his hand.

More importantly, she didn't step away.

They walked slowly. Country music rose and fell as people opened what he imagined was the door to the neighborhood bar. He didn't see one vehicle that wasn't a truck of some kind, or an SUV. And he only noticed that because he forced himself to think of something other than what it would be like to touch a hell of a lot more than her elbow.

Maybe it was the mystery that made him feel this powerful pull, but he doubted that was all. He remembered sitting in his Dallas bedroom at one point, her file spread in front of him, thinking that he might have liked her if she'd been the person she appeared to be.

Now that he'd met her, she was more that woman than he could have imagined. Hardworking, dedicated, kind, strong. It didn't hurt that she pressed all his personal preference buttons in terms of her looks, but this thing, it wasn't just physical.

He really liked Annie. More than he should, that's for damn sure. It was wrong to feel like this when she'd done so much damage to his brother, but he couldn't seem to help himself. So what, was he trying to justify his reaction to her, is that why he was finding it increasingly hard to believe she was capable of such a crime? Not an easy pill to swallow. Though both scenarios were troubling.

If what his gut told him about Annie was right, he had to seriously consider that Christian hadn't told the full truth about the embezzlement. Or flat out lied. Oh, man, that wasn't a possibility Tucker wanted to entertain at all. His mother would crumble.

But that changed nothing, because with every conversation, his certainty that Annie's guilt would be mitigated grew. He slid her a look that went unnoticed. With an upward tilt of her lips she was busy gazing at the clear blue sky. She loved Safe Haven, loved this small corner of Montana. Annie was doing good for the animals and the community without expectation of personal gain. It wasn't just him—the people who worked alongside her believed that.

Dammit, he wasn't wrong about her. And that wasn't his lower half talking.

She stopped, and it startled him, but then he saw the beat-up green truck of hers.

He moved around to face her, reluctantly releasing his hold. "Thank you for coming to dinner with me."

She shrugged. "As Shea would say, I really do want your money."

"Is that it? The only reason you came tonight?"

"Not completely. I admit, I find you good company. You were helpful yesterday, and I didn't properly thank you for that. Today, you asked intelligent questions, and I could see you care deeply about what your foundation does. You listened to me. Heard me. I appreciate that."

"You're fascinating. I would probably have listened to you read the phone book, although that wouldn't have been nearly as interesting as hearing about your plans for the shelter." He put his attraction to her out there, then watched closely, waiting for a small tell. A sign that she knew he was ripe for the picking, a perfect mark. One sultry smile and she could have him reaching for his checkbook....

"Thanks." She blinked. "I think."

He paused, knowing he should go. Right now. Just say good-night and walk away. "Annie," he said, his voice lower, soft enough for her to lean forward. "You're—"

She moistened her lips. "I'm...?"

He kissed her, half hoping to uncover the ruthless Warner woman who'd turned so many lives upside down. But it was sweet Annie Sheridan who kissed him back.

9

THE PRESSURE OF HIS LIPS STOLE far more than Annie's breath. She found herself leaning on him, as if to hold herself up and also to make sure this wasn't all in her head. He was solid against her, strong enough to carry her, and she'd been alone so long, shouldering everything.

A moment later, she parted her lips, opened her mouth in invitation, urging him to enter. He tasted incredible, nothing she could point to like beer or chocolate…it was more masculine than that. Maybe it was his clean scent— he'd showered and changed and this was him without hay and goats and horseflesh.

Her moan rose as he ran his hand under her hair. He cupped the nape of her neck, holding her steady while he changed his angle, and kissed her so thoroughly she shook with the need for more.

Gripping his upper arms, she made sure he didn't move while she pressed against him, her right breast, her thigh. His hand slid down her back, stilling in the small curve above her behind. Then he pulled her closer, and it was so overwhelming her head fell back as she gasped.

"No," he said, kissing her jaw, the curve of her neck, then back up until he found her mouth again. A quick nip on her bottom lip was followed by a thrust of his tongue, then a whisper of breath without touching at all as if they were trying out kisses to see what fit. Every one of them was perfect.

Each kiss and touch brought increased awareness that she was tasting Tucker, that the moments she'd imagined in her fantasies were becoming reality. She'd let him break the shell of her abstinence, and she knew the amazing shocks running through her body, making her squeeze her legs together, would cost her.

Dizzy with greed, she let the thought go, chased it away when she pried one hand free so she could touch his chest. If only she could reach under his shirt, feel his skin and hair and run her tongue over his nipples and hear the sounds he'd make.

Instead, like a cell door closing, approaching laughter slammed between them. She jumped away from him so quickly she almost tripped.

Tucker steadied her with his large hands. Thank God the lighting in the back lot was crap because her face felt as if it was on fire. The laughing people had nearly reached them, and she hoped they didn't recognize her.

"I should let you get home," Tucker said, releasing her completely.

She nodded. "The board meeting's at one o'clock. At Sadie's Watering Hole. The bar. It's impossible to miss, seeing as it's the only one."

"Ah, holding the meeting where there's alcohol. Attendance should be good."

She got the truck keys from her jeans' pocket. "Oh, you have no idea. The board members are…eclectic."

"I look forward to it. You don't need me to come in the morning? To Safe Haven, I mean?"

"You don't have to, no. I mean, if you want to…"

"I should use the time to take care of some business."

She looked at him, only then realizing she'd kept her head down since they'd stopped kissing. "Of course. Okay, then. I'll see you tomorrow."

He leaned forward as if to kiss her again, but she sidestepped him and grabbed hold of the truck door handle. Luckily, he caught himself in time and moved away so smoothly no one would have ever guessed his true intent.

"Night."

He distanced himself further. "Good night."

Her fingers shook when she tried to insert the key into the ignition, but she made it out of the parking lot without mishap. He was in her rearview mirror until she turned onto Main Street.

Regret didn't truly hit until she reached the highway.

For the third time in the past fifteen minutes, Tucker had to reread the email from his attorney. The memory of Annie in his arms kept intruding. Followed swiftly by recrimination and doubt.

It was a quarter to eleven, mere hours from when he'd kissed her, and despite the work that was piling up and his assistant becoming increasingly hysterical over Tucker's botched schedule, he couldn't get his thoughts straight and figure this mess out. Because he'd crossed a line, for better and for worse.

First and foremost, there was no doubt in his mind that the woman he'd kissed was not some criminal mastermind who'd willfully stolen money that should have gone to charity. However, a lot of questions remained unanswered, and that bothered him.

He was determined to clear his brother's name, absolutely, but now he wanted even more to understand everything that had happened to the funds and who was behind the embezzlement.

Was there more he could be doing on that score? He put his head in his hands, waited for a brainstorm, for something he'd missed, but George was following up on every thread Tucker had found.

Second, Tucker wasn't going to inform the D.A. about finding Leanna Warner until he not only understood what had happened, but had evidence to back up the truth. Period. He was not going to wrench her away from Safe Haven until they had some solid information…enough, at least, to get her out of hot water and to clear Christian's reputation. He may not be able to stay with her until he and George put together a complete picture. But he had his own plane, and flying to Montana wasn't a hardship. And with telecommuting, he could work from practically anywhere.

Which reminded him that he had to call his mother in the morning, even before he called to check in with George. What Tucker wasn't sure about was letting her or Christian in on what was happening.

No, he'd stick with his decision. The fewer people who knew about Annie, the better. For now. She wasn't going anywhere. Not with a new foal coming. And she'd never desert the animals. Not unless her back was up against the wall. He'd seen how much she cared in her eyes, in her plans, in her passion. But more than that, he'd seen it in her actions.

There was so much to distrust about people. Words were easy and glib and to trust blindly was an idiot's game. Tucker might be a fool for wanting Annie so badly, but he wasn't being stupid about who she was.

He believed in her. And he would be proven right.

He opened his eyes as an idea came to him. He wouldn't

decide yet whether to act on it, but it was interesting. Very interesting.

His cell, already plugged in and charging, rang. His mother's name came up on his display, and he couldn't hit Talk fast enough. It was late, Texas time. "Mom?"

"Are you coming home tomorrow?" she asked quietly.

"No, I'm not. I'm sorry. I'm not certain when I can be back."

"I see."

Her sigh felt like a slap. The only kind she would give him, the kind that hurt deep and long. "Did you go out with Andrea tonight?"

"No." Her quiet shudder echoed in her voice. "She wanted to go for sushi and you know how I feel about that."

"I do," he said. "Did you watch a movie?"

"I think so. If I did, it wasn't particularly memorable. The house creaked a lot. I thought…"

"Were you frightened?"

"Only a little. I let Martha go home early."

Tucker stood, wishing he could do more, but he couldn't drop this thing with Annie on the off chance he could make his mother feel better. He understood that grief took all kinds of shapes, that time was relative when it came to mourning. He still felt it himself. He'd loved his father. Missed him. He could have used his old man's thoughts on this Christian business, but if Michael had still been alive, Tucker had no idea if he and his mother would be involved with Christian at all.

The thought made him ashamed, and that combined with his guilt at leaving her on her own felt like a physical weight on his back. "While I'm away, don't send the staff home early, all right? Not even Martha."

"I don't even know where you are," Irene said. "Not Dallas."

"Montana, actually."

"Do we know people there?"

"We do, but that's not why I'm here." He hesitated, knowing in his gut it wasn't a good idea to tell her anything at this juncture. She'd have too many questions he couldn't answer. But at least she'd have something to hang on to, and perhaps then he wouldn't feel so damn guilty. "Now, don't get your hopes too high, but it's possible I may have found Leanna Warner."

Her inhale stopped him. "Oh, Tucker."

"It's not certain," he said, hating the necessary lie. "Nothing is. George is working with me, and we'll just have to see how this plays out."

"But if it is her Christian will be so happy. The D.A. will leave him be. He'll be able to go back to work, wherever he chooses. He could work in Dallas. We could help him find something. You know so many people in the financial world. Oh, Tucker, this will be wonderful."

His mistake didn't take long to bite him in the ass. "Mom, I don't know if it's her. Not for sure. She *may* be the woman we're looking for. Please, don't get carried away, not yet. It's just, we can hope, right? I have to ask you not to mention this to Christian. The last thing I want is for him to—"

"Yes, yes. It's not a done deal. I'm depressed, sweetheart, not stupid. I understand completely. But thank you. I needed a bit of hope today."

"I'm sorry I'm not there."

"No. Now that I know what you're doing, I'll be fine. Whatever the outcome. You're trying. It means a great deal."

"I am trying." Out of the blue, he thought of the kiss and his chest tightened. "Look, I'll call you as soon as I can. Tomorrow, if possible."

"Be careful. I think this woman must be very clever if she could have fooled Christian. Slippery, too."

He closed his eyes at her words, wishing he could tell her everything, how she would like Annie if only she got to know her. How it would be as clear as day that there was more to the story.

Instead, he said goodbye and hung up, not dialing George right away. Annie was clever. Which was part of the reason he believed in her so resolutely.

Tomorrow afternoon he'd prove it to her.

ANNIE, HOLDING A BOX OF FILE folders, pulled open the door to the Watering Hole half an hour before the meeting would start. The jukebox was quiet, the bar deserted because it wouldn't open until four, although she knew Sadie had to be around somewhere. She didn't leave the door unlocked if she left anymore.

There'd been a rash of thefts in Blackfoot Falls last summer, which sadly had turned out to be perpetrated by locals. But it just went to show that people were people, whether they lived in New York or the wilds of Montana.

She walked across the wooden floor, her eye catching on the beautiful Wurlitzer. She wished it held more music that she liked instead of mostly country songs, but it didn't really matter since she hardly ever came in here.

Lounging around and having drinks with friends felt like something she'd read about in a book. So many things had gone away, vanished in a haze of panic and shame. A manicure would be laughable considering how she spent her days, let alone a pedicure. In Manhattan she'd often saved up for a spa day, not the high-end deals, of course, but a soothing massage, a facial. God, to be pampered like that was unthinkable now.

"Hey there, girl. Thought you'd be coming in early. Good to see you."

Annie swung around at Sadie's rusty voice. Every time Annie had seen her in the past few months, the older woman had lost a bit more weight, used a touch more makeup, including lipstick this time. "You look wonderful."

"Yeah, I'm a stunner." Sadie came up to Annie, but knowingly didn't reach out for a hug.

"Hey, none of that." Annie surprised herself and Sadie by briefly touching her arm. "I think Shea's going to be here soon, too, but the big news is that we have a potential donor coming to the meeting."

"Really? Think that's wise?"

"I've warned him. And he understands that the board members are locals doing a nice thing for the animals. I think it'll be fine. I hope. As long as Abe and Will don't get into it."

"They do and I'll knock their fool heads together. Come on, let's get these tables set up. You want something to drink?"

"No, thanks." Annie put the box on the huge mahogany bar, then helped Sadie push the small tables into a big rectangle. Halfway through moving the chairs, Shea walked in.

No hello or other pleasantry. "Is he still planning on attending?" Shea asked.

Annie nodded, while Sadie appeared unfazed. People were getting used to Shea's blunt ways.

"According to some," Sadie said, darting an amused look at Annie, "you were at Marge's last night with the best-looking man seen in Blackfoot Falls since Paul Newman visited town forty years ago."

Annie hated the fact that her cheeks filled with heat. "His name is Tucker Brennan, and don't you dare let people start rumors about him. He's rich, and he's got a foundation that could be the salvation of Safe Haven. Anything else about him is nobody's business."

"Whoa," Sadie said, holding up her hands. "I wasn't implying anything."

"I know people in this town live for gossip but I don't know what I'd do if somebody's stupid remark screwed this up."

Sadie touched Annie's shoulder. "I understand. I'll do my best to derail any talk."

After releasing her pent-up breath, Annie sighed. "Thanks. And sorry for getting worked up."

"Don't you fret." Sadie turned to greet Jesse, who'd walked in, then she herded Shea behind the bar to help fill mugs.

Beer, Annie had learned early, came automatically with all meetings that took place in the Watering Hole. Annie was used to it, but she wondered what Tucker would make of it.

Just talking about him had set her body all aflutter, and she had to tamp down her excitement. This was no time to act like a silly girl. This could be the most important few hours since she'd come to Blackfoot Falls. Something that would set her up for a future she had more than accepted. She belonged at Safe Haven, and every day spent working there chipped away at the guilt and pain of what she'd left behind.

Abe, the owner of Abe's Variety, and notorious for his unrequited crush on Sadie, walked in right ahead of Will Woodruff, who was pretty partial to Sadie himself. What they had in common did not bring the two men closer together, to say the least. Even though their scowls were a matched set.

In silence, they headed for the back room where Jesse was scrounging more chairs.

Cy Heber joined them, and he would always make Annie smile because he'd donated four acres to Safe Haven, bless him. He was an old cowboy who gave a damn, who wanted to leave something good behind, even though his own ranch was a shadow of its former self.

The door opened one more time, and Tucker Brennan walked in wearing a fine-looking Stetson along with dark pressed jeans, a pale blue Oxford shirt and a navy blazer. She bit her bottom lip, not because he filled the doors with his broad shoulders, but because of the smile that lit up his face the moment he saw her.

"Oh…okay," Sadie murmured as she put four beers down on the table. "So they weren't exaggerating."

"Hush," Annie whispered as she went to welcome him, trying her best not to mentally replay last night's kisses.

It didn't take long for everyone to take their seats and for Annie to make introductions. She sat Tucker at one end of the table, and she took her place at the other. Which might have been a mistake from the way she kept getting caught on his gaze.

But somehow she managed to begin the meeting in what was considered parliamentary procedure for Blackfoot Falls. Everybody raised and seconded everything. At least at the start.

Up until she called for new business. That's when Tucker stood. Took off his hat. Reached into his jacket pocket and pulled out a slip of paper.

"I've been spending some time at Safe Haven, and I'm very impressed with the operation. I've seen facilities with much more do a lot less. I applaud you all for doing your part for animals in need." He paused, glanced around at everyone, but settled his gaze on Annie. "This is a check.

It's not from the Rocking B Foundation. I don't make the call on who gets foundation funds. This is a personal check, one that I hope will help as you continue to develop the sanctuary. There are no strings attached—it's to be spent at your discretion."

He walked around the table and handed the check to Annie. When she looked at it, she gasped at the amount. Twenty thousand dollars. What she could do with twenty grand was more than she could comprehend. She blinked up at Tucker, then turned to the others. "We can get the engine. We can fix the tractor." She looked again at the check to make sure she wasn't crazy, then back at Tucker.

"I believe in what you're doing," he said. "I believe in you."

Annie's heart nearly stopped. His message was completely heartfelt in its honesty. She'd have been thrilled beyond measure if only he'd stopped with that first sentence. Because believing in her was believing a lie.

10

"WELL, I SAY WE USE THE REST of the money to build a quarantine barn," the gray-haired gent who owned the variety store said, his big hand almost dwarfing his beer mug.

Tucker spared him a glance, but only that. The same was true for the others. He only had eyes for one person, and it killed him that he'd had no choice but to return to his seat at the far end of the table. Since it would've been highly inappropriate to kiss her in the middle of the board meeting. He'd settle for staring into her gorgeous blue eyes.

"We should invest in some of them big internet sales things." This from another old man, Cy Heber, who looked as worn as the creaking weather vane atop the Safe Haven barn. "Those ads just keep on popping up no matter what, so they're bound to get folks' attention."

"Heber, that's spam," Jesse said, doing an admirable job of keeping a straight face. "Besides, we're already doing two internet campaigns."

Tucker watched as Annie finally put the check in her pocket and focused her entire attention on him. But instead of the heated glances from before, she seemed more confused than the money warranted. He would've liked her to smile at least, but he figured she was having mixed feelings.

He wanted her to know he was on her side. No matter what happened later with the information George gathered, where the chips fell, he needed Annie to believe that he had faith in her. That check meant something to him, as well. He never had been and never would be cavalier about his wealth, inherited or earned. Damn, he couldn't wait until there were no more secrets between them. But for now, he hoped his gesture would ease her mind in some small way.

The older cowboy, Will, said, "I think we should hire someone who can be there for Annie so that she doesn't have to work three hundred sixty-five days a year. A person needs to have some time off."

That made Annie turn. "I don't need any such thing."

Everyone started talking at once, except for Shea, who just shook her head. In fact, she'd said very little since the meeting started forty minutes ago.

Sadie slammed her hands down on the table so hard and loud she brought the chatter to a halt. "Quiet, all of you. What we're gonna do with that check is just what we've done with every other donation. Leave it to Annie. She knows better than all of us combined what Safe Haven needs. And if you don't agree, I'm bringing this meeting to a close right this second, and you can all pay for your own damn beer."

Finally, Tucker got his smile from Annie.

ANNIE WANTED TO HUG SADIE for stopping the free-for-all the board meeting had become. It was torture sitting with all these people. It was no picnic sitting across from Tucker, either.

The check and all it meant hadn't truly hit yet. Big ideas like gratitude and what she could do with so much money were right beside the echo of his words, his belief in her that made her want to weep until next week.

If he knew the truth, would he have been so quick to give her anything? No, of course not. Who would? But then, his generosity hadn't been toward Leanna Warner, and she couldn't forget that. The whole point of staying in Safe Haven was to do everything in her power to help the cause. To hide her mistakes in a coffee can under her bed, and dedicate her days and hours to something worthwhile.

The smart thing would be to continue on as if nothing had changed. In truth, nothing had. Except for the extra-large infusion of guilt.

Oh, and wanting Tucker so badly she found it hard to breathe.

She'd agonized for hours last night and before the meeting, berating herself for kissing him when there was so much at stake. Intellectually she knew that Tucker wasn't using his position to manipulate her, and she wasn't trying to use their attraction for her own benefit. But the check and the confirmation that the foundation would make an independent decision took care of any lingering doubts.

Forcing herself to tie up the meeting, to actually speak to Will and Cy and the rest of the board and really listen, put more strain on her than she'd have guessed. Tucker was there, right there, and every step closer made her want him more.

Shea and Jesse lingered after the others had left, taking the time to thank Tucker and to ask him what kind of receipt he'd like for the donation.

Annie figured that would be it. Because she had a hell of a lot to do.

"You going back to Safe Haven?" Shea asked.

Annie shook her head. "I'd like to go to Kalispell and deposit the check. Tucker's bank has a branch there. Maybe

I can keep out enough money for the engine so we can order it today. Spring will be gone before we know it."

Tucker, who'd been speaking to Jesse, joined Shea and Annie. "I could take you to the bank. Make sure you get whatever cash you need."

"No, that's okay," Annie said, ordering herself not to be nervous just because he was a foot away. "I'll have to get back to Safe Haven tonight, and you don't want to make all those trips. Not if you're leaving tomorrow."

"I'm a damn good customer of that bank. If I'm with you, they'll let you have the whole check in cash if you want." He smiled, lifted his shoulder in a casual shrug. "And hey, maybe we could even splurge and get some dinner."

Annie sighed, knowing it would be dangerous to go to Kalispell with Tucker. She'd already proven that she had no defense against this man, and God knew, she'd already broken almost every rule in her book. Still, the tractor had been sitting there for so long, and the kids had worked so hard on the project. She looked up at Shea. "Do you think you might be able to cover for me for a few hours?"

Shea smiled. "I know I can."

Jesse moved next to her. "Me, too." Then, weirdly, he nudged Shea in her side. He tried not to be obvious, but Annie saw it. Her pulse jumped when Jesse asked Tucker to join him outside.

"Maybe you should take a toothbrush with you," Shea said.

"What!" Annie groaned. Dammit, someone must've seen the kiss last night. "Are you crazy?"

Despite the flush on her cheeks, Shea took a step closer to Annie and leaned in. "Maybe get some underwear. Abe's Variety has both, you know. Then you wouldn't have to drive back to Safe Haven." Shea smiled. "Jesse and I can stay as long as you need us to. Honest."

Annie could hardly believe Shea's suggestion, and Jesse's part in this little maneuver. She wished she'd never kissed Tucker. No. That he'd never kissed her. Did everyone in the county know about it? Could a rumor spread that fast?

What was she thinking? This was Blackfoot Falls. Of course it could. Even worse, the kiss wasn't a rumor. It probably hadn't helped that she and Tucker had been ogling each other during the meeting. Jeez, she'd never live this down. Never.

Luckily, what the people of this tiny town thought of her wasn't high on her list of things she cared about. Tucker was. So was his imminent departure. God, why did she have to like him so much? Men simply did not make her heart pound anymore. Or send heat surging through her veins. But then she hadn't met anyone like him before. In her experience, rich, powerful men didn't give up their valuable time to help bring a foal into the world or get their hands dirty saving a helpless goat.

Even though she didn't deserve to be with a man like him, the fact that this was it, that they'd never see each other again once he left, was eating at her resolve faster than the summer sun melted a Popsicle. Her priorities had shifted even as she tried to reason with herself. He'd already given her a check, no strings attached, and the foundation was a separate entity. One obstacle out of the way. Was that why he'd chosen the meeting to present the check? It didn't matter. In her heart she knew… She needed tonight with Tucker as much as she needed the tractor to work.

Maybe more.

"You're right, I should duck into Abe's," she said, having trouble meeting Shea's gaze. "If you're sure."

"Please." Shea rolled her eyes. "Even I could tell you guys wanted to crawl all over each other."

Annie felt her own blush. "Oh."

"Yeah. Hurry up. I'll be talking to Tucker about when we should expect to hear from the foundation."

Annie wanted to hug her, but instead she waved at Sadie across the room, then darted out the door, ready and willing to head into a night she'd never forget. And hang the consequences.

TUCKER WAS ABOUT AS PLEASED with himself as a man could be. He had an amazing woman sitting at his side and the promise of a perfect night of nothing but spoiling her rotten in every way he could think of. Mostly, he hoped, by giving her many, many orgasms.

He'd never have asked Annie to spend the night with him. At best, he'd hoped she might ask him into her cabin after the volunteers left in the evening. But then Shea and Jesse had offered their help, and Annie had disappeared into the variety store. There were enough clues in her body language to let him know she'd picked up a few essentials. When Shea said, "See you tomorrow," the deal was sealed in his mind.

"I can't begin to thank you for the generous check, Tucker," Annie said as they merged onto the highway. "Your faith in Safe Haven won't be misplaced, I swear."

Tucker gave her a look that was a little too smug.

"I'm being sincere," Annie said.

His expression softened at her offended tone, and he realized what she must think. "Sorry. I know you are. I meant no offense. It's just…I've been caught up thinking about all the things I want to do after you take care of business. Things I want to do with you." He reached across the SUV and took her hand. "For you."

"Oh," she said, after a few seconds. "Carry on, then."

He laughed. "I intend to." After a quick squeeze, he returned his hand to the wheel because he'd been waiting for a place to pull over. There was no traffic to speak of, and he had no trouble moving onto the shoulder.

"What's wrong?" she asked. "Is it the car?"

"The SUV is fine," he said, driving onto a patch of gravel and away from the two-lane road. "What's wrong," he said, killing the engine and turning to Annie, "is that I haven't kissed you since last night."

Undoing his seat belt, he leaned over, mentally cursing bucket seats and intrusive consoles, and slipped his hand behind Annie's neck. He didn't have to pull her close; she came eagerly to meet him in the middle.

She skipped tentative altogether and went straight for mind-blowing with a quick but insistent swipe of her tongue, vanquishing any doubts he'd had about the true purpose of this escape.

He couldn't have stopped his groan if he'd tried. That he remembered her taste, that her scent had already become vital, made him glad he'd closed his eyes, because looking at her now would make him want far more than a kiss.

The moment her hand touched his chest, he gripped her more firmly, took over the kiss and slipped his tongue between her teeth. Her whimper excited his already stirring cock, and as they explored each other, the sounds of their desire filled the interior of the cab, making everything more intense.

Her roving hand reminded him that he could touch now, touch more than he'd dared last night. If the pull of actually getting her into bed hadn't been so enticing, he might have listened to the voice in the back of his head reminding him the back of the Land Rover was roomy, and how no cars had driven by since he'd pulled over.

Instead, he cupped her breast with his left hand. Over her shirt, over her bra. And learned the shape of her, the feel of her against his palm. This wasn't a grope and dash… it was a prelude, something to take the edge off until he could give her the perfect setting. Although his body wasn't too thrilled with the decision.

She drew back just as he was marveling at how hard her nipple was through two layers. "We should probably go."

Giving in, he opened his eyes, and dammit, the look of her lips, all moist and pink, was enough to make him hard. "You all right?"

"Better than all right. But I want—"

"Everything?"

She smiled, kissed him quickly on the lips, then sat back in her seat, pulling her seat belt across her chest. "Think we can do everything in one night?"

"We can sure as hell try," he said, then he put the car in gear and turned back onto the freeway, the memory of her kisses lingering like the slow, pleasant burn of twenty-year-old Scotch.

"WHEN I WAS SEVEN, I WANTED to be a fireman."

Annie immediately pictured him in one of those sexy calendars, wearing all of his gear except for his shirt. He'd have made the cover for sure. "What happened to change your mind?"

"Batman."

"Really? How's that working out for you?"

He grinned. "Great. Although the commute to Gotham is killing me."

She turned more toward him, feeling as if she were in a dream, because this was not her life. Every time she started to sink back to reality, the one she'd find soon enough in Blackfoot Falls, she snapped herself out of it. She'd have the rest of her life for regrets. But she wouldn't begin now. "I hope you brought your alter ego with you, because I'm thinking you'd look seriously hot in tights."

His laughter was deep and real and made her shiver. It also made her touch him. Her hand on his. Nothing major, no groping. The last thing she wanted was to distract him from getting them to the bank. And the hotel. She really wanted to be at that hotel.

"I can guarantee that you will never see me wearing tights. In fact, you need to stop thinking about it right now."

"Hey, tights can be very manly. All the best superheroes wear them."

Tucker looked at her. "No, some of them wear jeans and checkered blouses."

Absurdly, she looked down, although she knew what she'd put on this afternoon. "Stop it," she said, meaning it. The last thing she needed to do was get mired in her mistakes again. In fact, she wasn't going to think about herself at all. "I want to know what happened after the Batman phase."

"That's easy. Ranching. Riding. Learning the ropes. Literally."

"Did you ever try the rodeo?"

"Not for long. Being thrown off a horse hurts like a son of a bitch."

"I doubt you experienced it often."

"Not something you should bet on." His mouth twisted into a wry smile. "I preferred playing baseball. Which I did through my sophomore year in college."

"Pitcher?"

"How'd you know?"

"I'm not sure," she said. "I had a feeling, that's all."

"Well, you're right. I started out in Little League. Eventually I developed a decent arm."

He flipped his hand over hers, entwined their fingers and rubbed the skin he could reach with his thumb. A tiny movement that resonated down to her toes.

"What about you? Horses all the way?"

"Mostly. I did play basketball in school. I was tall enough to be a guard, but definitely not good enough to continue past high school. The love of my life has always been horses, though."

"No men on that list?"

She shook her head. "I lived with a guy for a few years. Thought it was love. Turned out it was more about lust and wishful thinking. Then, I don't know. Nothing major. A few mistakes. How about you?"

"I've had several relationships through the years. I expected to be married by now. I'd like to have kids. Raise them on the ranch like my father raised me. But the women that have interested me the most have had busy lives and goals of their own."

"The twain couldn't meet?"

"Five days a week I live on the ranch. I spend the weekends in Dallas. For a professional woman, that's a hard schedule to work around. And it would be difficult at the moment to give up my role at the ranch."

They were getting closer to Kalispell and traffic had picked up. She didn't want to think about him getting married and having kids. She didn't want to think of him outside of this car.

She shifted so she could see him better. "Tell me about the hotel room. Does it have a big bathtub?"

Like the gentleman he was, Tucker let the subject turn to exaggerations about the room's amenities. She relaxed against her seat, watching him as he spoke, studying that strong jaw of his before getting swept away by his cheekbones.

When the town came into view, she was a little disappointed. The ride had been the easiest stretch of time she'd had in so long. A snapshot of a life she'd never have.

FIVE MINUTES AFTER TUCKER and Annie walked into the Kalispell branch of Tucker's bank, his phone rang, and the name surprised him. He answered quickly with, "Hang on, I'll just be a minute," then turned to Annie. "I shouldn't be long, but I have to take this."

"Go ahead. If I need you to get the money, I'll wait, that's all. No problem."

He leaned over but ended up kissing her cheek instead of her mouth. She seemed as surprised as he was. He knew it was a reaction to the phone call, but he'd think about the reason later.

He didn't speak to Christian until he was in the back parking lot, away from too many passersby and far from where Annie could overhear. "What's going on, Christian?"

"That's what I want to know," his brother said.

The bite behind his words had Tucker stopping in his tracks. "You'll have to be more specific."

"Why the hell didn't you tell me you were looking for Leanna?"

"Because I don't report to you," Tucker said, instantly angry both at his impudent brother and his mother. Though he still didn't know what she'd told Christian. "Did Mom call you?"

"Yes, *Irene* called." Christian often used her name to emphasize the fact he hadn't yet forgiven her. Though he didn't mind taking her money. "She informed me you found Leanna."

"I'm not sure yet that I have. But if it is her, what are you complaining about?"

"I'm complaining because I had my own search going for her. I didn't want you involved. Leanna is a dangerous woman."

"In what way?" Tucker gritted his teeth. Getting pissed off wouldn't help. But Annie, dangerous? "You said she was a thief. That she'd taken off with the money."

Christian's huff came through as impatience, but Tucker heard more than that. Underneath the anger was panic. But over what? "Look, I didn't tell you because I didn't see the point, but there were some very shady and dangerous people in Leanna's life. People associated with the mob. Guys you don't want to get too close to, you understand? They could come after you, Tucker. And Mom."

The mob and Annie? Is that why she'd run, why she'd hidden herself away in a backwoods town near the border? Jesus, if Christian had known about it… "Why didn't you tell the police?"

"Because I didn't particularly want to die. I told you, these men are lethal. Hell, even if it is Leanna, you wouldn't be doing her any favors by bringing her in. That would be as good as signing her death warrant. Leave it alone, Tucker. This is something your big money can't fix. Trust me."

"If you'd told me the—" Tucker cut himself short. How could he blame Christian for trying to protect himself? For protecting his family? "Fine. I won't do anything to endanger you. Or her. If it is her."

"Don't say anything to anyone about this, Tucker. I'm dead serious. It won't end well."

"I understand." Tucker had walked to the side of the bank, and was headed for the entrance. He poked his head inside the door and saw Annie standing in the waiting area.

"Where are you, anyway? Mom didn't say."

Now it was Mom. Tucker wasn't sure why that rubbed

him the wrong way, but it sure as hell did. "Flying back to Dallas. I've got to run. I'll be in touch when I get home." Tucker put the phone away, more worried than ever about Annie. And Christian, yeah, but his brother seemed to be pretty good at taking care of himself.

He'd have to wait until he took Annie to order the tractor engine before he called George, see what he'd found out. Warn him. God, he hoped he hadn't sent George into danger. The thought made him so uncomfortable that after he helped Annie get her funds, he made another excuse to leave her to deal with the salesman at the machinery parts store. But she didn't just let him slip away.

"Is everything okay?"

He put on a smile, hating the subterfuge. "It's business, a fire I have to put out myself. It won't take long."

"I'll be here, and I don't mind waiting. So do what you need to." Then she pulled his head down to meet her in a kiss.

Not just a peck, either. It didn't matter that they were standing inside a busy warehouse. She took her time, and he let himself enjoy it. It hit him that he'd been one hundred percent right about her from the moment they'd met. No, from before that. He'd read her perfectly. Someone else was behind the embezzlement and had forced her hand. The only problem was, now that he understood the danger she was in, would trying to help her make things worse?

He pulled back to rest his forehead against hers, held her there for a long moment as he breathed her in, calmed himself down. There would be a solution to this. He would find one. Because anything else was unacceptable.

A few minutes later, he was on the phone with George, who delivered news Tucker wasn't prepared to hear. He found a wall to lean against. "Wait. Bookies?"

"Major bookies," George said. "These guys are affiliated with the Russian mob, Tucker. I'm sorry, but the trail is there."

"You're sure it leads to Christian?"

"No. I'm not," George said in a slow, cautious voice. "But so far, that's where things are headed."

"George, look, I appreciate everything you've done, but you need to stop now. Just back off. This is far bigger than I ever expected, and I won't have you put yourself in this kind of danger."

"You need to trust me on this, my friend. I'm not willing to get involved in anything that could get me killed. Or you, or Irene. But I've got a lifetime of sources here, and a lot of favors I've called in. I'm fine, and I'll stay fine. And I'm not stopping. If I can clear your brother, I will. But know this. I won't pull any punches."

Tucker rubbed the back of his neck. "If Irene knew, she'd be as grateful as I am. But she'd also be just as worried. No more burials, George. Not over this. Not worth it."

"I couldn't agree more. I'll get back to you."

Tucker turned off the phone, and shoved it in his pocket. Bookies. There'd been nothing in Annie's life or financial history that would tie her to gambling of any sort. Nothing. He couldn't say the same for Christian.

Jesus, what if…? No, he wouldn't jump to conclusions. The idea that Christian could be involved with the embezzlement had crossed his mind before—Tucker wasn't an idiot—but he'd dismissed the notion.

The reason for that was clear. He just hoped like hell he wasn't going to be responsible for hurting his mother even more than she was already. In the middle of forcing a deep breath, it finally struck him why he'd been annoyed that Christian switched from Irene to Mom. Subconsciously he'd recognized it had been a tactic. Pure manipulation. To tug at Tucker's emotions by upping the stakes. Even if

Tucker didn't care about himself, Christian knew he'd care about what happened to Irene. He'd back off then.

The question remained…why? Did Christian truly believe Leanna Warner was involved with the mob and feared for his life? Or was he afraid she had information that would prove his own guilt?

Damn, everything had just gotten more complicated. He should never have come to Montana. But if he'd never come, he'd have never met Annie. She wasn't the dangerous woman his brother had painted her to be. Not possible.

He walked into the store and found her by the tractors. The second she took the copy of her purchase order, he pulled her into his arms and backed her away from the counter. "I should take you to dinner. You haven't eaten for hours."

"But…?"

He looked at her, wanting to tell her everything, wanting to hide her away where no one would ever hurt her. She wasn't guilty; he still believed that with every fiber of his being, every inch of his soul. And he wanted her more than he'd ever wanted any woman. "Are you really hungry?"

"Starving," she said, a slow, sexy smile lifting the corners of her lips.

He winced, but only for a second. "Want to go find a restaurant?"

"Not a chance. Where is this hotel of yours?"

11

THE HOTEL WASN'T CLOSE ENOUGH. They had to get into the car, drive for several blocks, find a place to park. By then, Annie's focus had shifted from deposits and new engines back to sex. Sex with this man. Not only had it been ages since she'd slept with anyone, the last time she'd had sex it had been only so-so. He'd been nice, and they'd hit it off pretty well over the course of several shared meals. But in bed? They hadn't gotten in sync. She'd sworn at the time that she was done with settling, that no man would get her into bed unless there was serious heat between them.

Tucker qualified. He kept stealing glances. She kept meeting his gaze. The sizzle should have steamed up the windows.

"What are you thinking?" she asked, as they walked from the parking lot, her toothbrush and a three-pack of ugly drugstore panties safely in her purse.

"That walking in my condition is awkward and a little painful."

"Blister from your boots?"

His arm around her shoulders tightened. "Yeah. A blister."

"I might have a blister myself. Smaller than yours, though."

"I should hope so."

Her stomach grumbled. Loudly. She put her hand on her belly. "Sorry about that."

"When's the last time you ate?"

"This morning. I had breakfast."

"Which consisted of…?"

"Hey, no playing Mom."

He bumped her hip with his. "That's not at all how I'm feeling at the moment, but I have seen your refrigerator. And your cupboards."

"Fine. I had toast and string cheese."

He brought them to a halt. "I'm feeding you."

"Yes, you are. Later."

"Not later. Now. I don't need you passing out during the best part."

She turned until she stood close enough to press against his "blister." "What precisely would the best part be?"

He kissed her, then moved his lips just far enough away from her to whisper, "All of it."

She captured his lower lip between her teeth, but let him go before he could object. "The gift shop has candy bars."

His green eyes looked darker staring at her from such close range, but she liked the view. Liked the man. "I feel like I'm not taking care of you properly."

"You can fix that the minute we get into your room."

"Why are we talking? We could be buying candy right this second."

She held on to his hand as they jogged to the back entrance and found the shop. She grabbed the first chocolate bar she saw, glad to see he picked one up, as well. Neither of them wasted a moment digging in, and they crumbled the wrapping in unison before the elevator opened at his floor.

Once she got inside the suite, the memory of her old life

hit fiercely. Thank goodness she had a legitimate excuse to shut herself into the bathroom. It was huge, but even the pleasure of seeing the big tub wasn't strong enough to stop the déjà vu.

Standing still as she looked into the mirror, she saw Leanna Warner. As the emotions welled in her throat, she clamped her eyes shut. "I'm here. Right now," she whispered. "With the most amazing man I've ever met, and I've got this one chance."

After a few deep breaths, she brushed her teeth and her hair, blessed whatever gods had made her shave her legs before going to the board meeting and went out the door wearing a smile that was turned electrically real the moment she saw him standing by the bed.

Just the way he looked at her made her nipples hard.

Tossing his Stetson on the couch, Tucker held her gaze as he slowly approached her. He wanted to watch her eyes darken the closer he got.

By the time he was a breath away, the blue of her irises had almost disappeared. "I can't decide whether I want to undress you piece by piece, or race you till we're both buck naked and panting."

"The second option gets my vote."

"Yeah?"

She nodded. Then she started unbuttoning her shirt, and the competition was on.

He won. Not the race—he'd lost that part. She was down to her underwear while he was still working on getting his boots off, but damn, the view was worth it.

"I'm pretty sure I'm the winner," she said, grinning, her thumbs hooked over the elastic of her panties.

"I could argue that." He knew she'd have great legs. "Want help?"

"No. I want to stare at you. It wouldn't hurt my feelings if you turned around a time or two."

She blushed. Pretty as a picture. The pink didn't stop with her cheeks, either. He was going to lick as much of that rosy skin as he could. Later. Taking his sweet time was for seconds. Not that he didn't want to impress her with his smooth moves, but he was already as hard as a bedpost just looking at her white cotton bra and panties.

One boot came off, and dammit, he had to focus for a minute on getting the second one loose. The moment he did, he shot to his feet and started working on his jeans.

When she did turn around, he nearly clipped himself with his zipper. Her body was even more amazing than he remembered, and he'd thought about it for two nights. Of course, he'd only seen that stretch of her back before, and now that he saw her behind, he knew he'd be dreaming of her for months, if not longer.

"Happy now?" she said, turning back to face him.

"Ecstatic," he said, and proved his point by dropping his jeans and boxer briefs at the same time. Then he realized his socks were still on, and he toed them off as fast as he was able. Almost fell over, but it was worth it.

She still laughed at him. Until he stood up tall, and then she got quiet. Seeing that look on her face as she stared down at him was a turn-on all by itself.

"Now you," he said, his voice lowering an octave.

He wanted to touch her as she reached behind her back to undo her bra clasp, but he kept his hands at his sides. Fisted, but still. His cock, not so much. The moment that bra fluttered to the floor, it jerked, tapping the flat of his stomach.

Annie was trembling slightly. Not like she was afraid. Just anxious. Her hands went to slide her panties off, and his plan to watch the whole show broke down. Before he knew he was going to do it, he hit his knees, inches away from her beautiful body.

She jumped, but didn't move back. When he looked up, he found her dark gaze and her tacit permission. He leaned forward, nestling his nose just below her indented belly button. She smelled so damn good, and she wasn't even unwrapped yet.

His fingers tugged her panties down slowly, and despite the impulse that urged him to speed the hell up, he unveiled her like a prize.

She had a perfect triangle of blond curls and once he'd uncovered her completely, he inhaled again. Nothing on earth compared to the scent of a woman, and he would swear on any book in the room that Annie had been designed with him in mind.

As gently as he could, he touched her inner thighs, hoping she'd get the hint. Bright and beautiful, she shifted her legs for him, and when he slipped two fingers just inside the barely parted lips, she was all moist heat and silk. It wasn't hard to find where she'd gotten hard, but he was careful with his touches. Still, one swipe made her grab onto his hair, a little more enthusiastically than he'd anticipated.

She let go immediately. "Sorry, I'm sorry."

Just the sound of her breathy apology got him hotter. "It's okay," he said, right before he blew a stream of air across where he'd touched.

"We need to rethink this," she said.

Talk about a cold shower. "What?"

"No…not…no. I can't do this standing up. I'm going to spoil everything if we don't get on the bed. Quickly."

Tucker obeyed like a shot. In fact, the second he was up, he had her in his arms. Not taking any chances, he swept an arm behind her knees and one across her back, lifted

her up and into a kiss as they crossed the short distance to
the bed. His romantic gesture crashed and burned when he
had to put her down to turn back the white spread.

Not that Annie seemed to mind. When she lay down,
she pulled him along and they picked up the kiss right
where they'd left off.

IT WASN'T EVEN FIVE-THIRTY, the room was filled with light
and precious space, and Annie had never felt more comfortable being naked with a man.

Maybe it was because he was clearly excited by her…
No, that wasn't a special feat in her experience. Perhaps
she'd given up being self-conscious when she'd given up
everything else. Her psyche seemed to realize that there
would be no return engagements.

Or it could just be that she liked him. So very much.
Something had clicked from that first meeting, and it had
never stopped. Despite her nerves and her secrets and her
endless responsibilities, she'd found him wonderful company. His touch… God, just now he was running his palm
up her side, then segueing to her breast, where he teased
her nipple as if she'd given him her personal instruction
manual.

She gasped, pulling away from his lips. Then they were
on her throat, in that sensitive spot below her ear. He didn't
just kiss, but licked and nibbled, and then when he murmured something indistinct the vibration kicked everything up a couple notches.

Easing her hand between them, she circled his length
and moved to the base and back up again.

He froze. Lips parted on her skin, tongue in midswipe.

He didn't even breathe as she repeated the motion, finding a rhythm that made her own heart pound.

Tucker made a garbled noise, half word, half moan, entirely unintelligible.

"You're welcome," she whispered, grinning before she nipped him on the earlobe.

"Annie. Annie. Annie."

Her grin became a laugh. "Yes, Tucker?"

"This is going to be over very quickly if you continue doing that."

She squeezed a little harder before she pumped him again. "You mean, this?"

"Yes," he said, through clenched teeth.

She sighed. "Sure, spoil all my fun." Letting him go, she was sorely tempted to go back for one more sneaky pull, but decided the consequences might not be to her liking.

"Later you have my full permission to carry on," he said. "But for now, let's at least go for ten minutes, okay?"

"I bet we can make it twenty, if we try."

He pushed up onto his arms until he was staring straight into her eyes. "Do you want me to have a stroke? Is that the plan?"

She liked this side of Tucker. Naked and pleading looked great on him. To show her appreciation, she wrapped her left leg over his lower back.

He closed his eyes for just a few seconds, and then pretended to glare at her. "You're a devil. A stunning devil, but still. You should be careful."

"Careful? Why? What's the worst that can happen?"

The right side of his mouth quirked up in one of her favorite smiles. "I might have to ravish you again and again."

Her other leg joined the first to reinforce that she was

in favor of that outcome. She used the traction to press up against his straining erection.

Watching him throw back his head as if he was already coming made her ache along with him. "Where did you put the condoms?"

"Give me a second. And don't move."

She didn't. Not a bit. At least, not with the obvious muscles.

A moment later, he took a deep breath, turned both of them to their sides until he could reach the bedside table. His weight was just getting to be too much for her when he rolled them back to their original position.

Then he sat up, unapologetically knocking her legs away. Annie held back a laugh, then watched him get ready. Goodness, he certainly looked impatient. But then so was she.

Once the condom was on, he leaned down again, and this time, he brought her legs up toward her chest. "Next time, I swear…" He stopped to kiss the inside of her ankle. "We'll have so much foreplay we'll both be wrecks."

"Sounds wonderful. Now what are you waiting for?"

He smiled and pushed inside her, one straight shot that had her arching her back and holding on for dear life.

It wasn't the most elegant sex she'd ever had, but it was exactly what she'd needed. She touched him wherever she could reach, hoped like hell the walls were thick or the room next door was empty, because she was not quiet.

The kisses that started out hot and deep ended up pants against each other's mouths, and it turned out that was about as sexy as anything she'd ever felt.

By the time he let her right leg go, and found her clit with his thumb, she was shaking and straining so hard she thought her heart would burst. Her orgasm crested before she had a chance to warn him. All she could do was hang on, muffle her scream with his shoulder and ride the wave.

When he pushed her whole body up the bed with the force of his thrust, she pulled her head back, opened her eyes. She watched him come, the intensity in his face breathtaking. When he could relax again, he smiled down at her, then pressed a soft kiss to her shoulder.

"Hell of an appetizer," he murmured.

Which made her stomach growl so loudly they laughed even as they collapsed in exhaustion.

TUCKER ONLY OPENED his menu after Annie caught his attention. She gave him the look that meant he'd better stop staring at her. Yes, that happened a lot, but this was different. She'd been studying Louie's deli menu as if it were the Rosetta Stone, and all her questions had been answered.

"A Reuben," she whispered, in a voice that was half awe, half hunger.

"Sauerkraut have some special meaning in your life?"

She looked again at the menu, then up at him. "The highlight of my month is eating in Marge's diner. Not that Marge's isn't swell—the food is great—but I think they missed the memo on what rye bread should taste like. And I'm not going to discuss their corned beef." She looked down again. "New York cheesecake. Please let that be true. Please."

Tucker had to grin, enjoying her excitement. But it also saddened him that he wanted to use her joy over New York food to press her about her old life. See if he couldn't find out something more, anything that would allow him to help her.

He couldn't think of a way to tell her what had brought him to Safe Haven without screwing everything up. Trying to convince her that he believed she was innocent and he was on her side wouldn't be enough. She'd be furious and frightened and would probably never trust him again.

That wasn't part of the plan. Even if he explained his about-face, she'd still know he'd lied to her. If their situations were reversed, he wouldn't believe anything that came out of her mouth.

All she was doing was trying to protect herself. And she'd done it by being a selfless defender to those that couldn't defend themselves. So what the hell should he do? Damn. If Christian had told the truth, and the mob was involved, Tucker's choices had narrowed considerably. His first priority was to keep her safe. Even if it meant she'd hate him forever.

"What's the matter? Are you okay?"

Pasting on a quick grin that became genuine as soon as he saw the concern in her eyes, he nodded. "I'm fine. Too many things look good. Like the Parmesan chicken sandwich. And the Bronx Bomber."

"That's the Philly cheese steak, right?"

He nodded. "So tell me. Carnegie Deli or Katz's?"

"That's a trick question. The pickles at Carnegie and the pastrami at Katz's. And how does a cowboy from Dallas know about Katz's, anyway?"

He shrugged. "Well, shucks, ma'am. I'm not rightly sure. But I think I hopped on that there subway train from Midtown to the Lower East Side, and there she was."

She ducked her head and looked at him through her lashes. "God, you're adorable."

"It's a burden, but one I've grown to accept."

The waitress came by to take their hefty order, but Annie still made the time to ball up her straw wrapper and throw it at his head. She had damn good aim, too.

The best part of the meal was hearing her make the

sounds he hoped to duplicate when they got back to the room.

The other great thing was her laughter. She seemed like a different person, sitting across the booth from him. No wonder. This was probably her first break in years, and it had been a revelation. Seeing her shed the burden of her responsibilities gave new light to her eyes, and when she smiled…

She made him forget, for long moments at a time, that he was unsure how to help both her and his brother, that his mother was walking on thin ice, that he had grown so used to being alone he'd learned to ignore the loneliness.

"Think we could stop here tomorrow before we head back home?"

"Sure." He wanted to sit here for hours, just staring, thinking about how her eyes matched the blue of the sky. "To eat here or carry out?"

She sighed, leaning back in the booth. "I'm taking home as much food as will fit into my fridge."

"That would be what, half a sandwich?"

She glowered. "There's another fridge in the stable, you know. A big one."

"I don't think you're supposed to put the cheesecake on the same shelf as the pergolide."

"Where there's a will…as they say."

"I'd be delighted to help you improve your stash. Frozen burritos? That's just not right."

Annie leaned forward. "Guess what? You do what you have to. Money's tight. And you know as well as I do that horses are accidents waiting to happen. Not to mention goats. I swear, they should have first-aid competitions at rodeos. I can wrap a blown kneecap in under a minute when necessary. And that includes any injections."

How was it possible to become even more impressed with this woman? And how quickly could he get her back to his hotel room?

12

"LET ME HELP YOU WITH THAT," Tucker said, walking toward Annie with a wicked smile.

"You're so thoughtful." She had already taken off her boots and socks and left them in the main room. The bath was filling quickly, the scent of lilacs hinted at summer gardens and would be forever imprinted with Tucker in her memory.

Unlike the first rush to push aside anything standing in the way of sex, he took his time unbuttoning her shirt. Would she have to get rid of these clothes once he left? Hide them in coffee cans so they wouldn't torment her?

She closed her eyes, forcing herself to be present, right here, right now. Why was it so difficult to stay in the moment with him? To experience every second as it was happening instead of jumping ahead?

After her shirt fell, she took hold of him. Instantly, she felt more grounded. Of course she'd have to let him go, but for now, contact was all important.

He'd been looking down at her chest, at her ugly bra, but then he shifted his gaze to her face, to her eyes. His touch halted as they met in a kiss. It was easy and sexy, and each time they parted lips, they kept hold of each other with their warm breath, and when they came back together it was a jolt of the best kind. Again and again, as if they were near a waterfall, lying in a meadow, alone in a steamy cave, all at once while never leaving the simple, spacious bathroom in an ordinary hotel.

Both of his hands, so strong and real, went to her bare waist and she came back to earth. He undid the buttons of her jeans as if he were popping champagne corks, and the image made her laugh.

"What?"

"Nothing. You. A bubble bath."

Just his smile did startling things to her. "Exciting, huh?"

"You have no idea. I have recurring dreams of taking long, luxurious soaks in perfectly scented water."

"Did they include a devilishly handsome man tending to your every need?"

She sighed as she leaned against him. "They will from now on."

"Good," he said, his lips close to her ear. "Keep that thought." Pulling away, he turned off the water, then came back to finish his task.

"I like that look."

She shook her head, not understanding.

"You, just like that. Your jeans open, bare feet."

"My retro bra?"

"Yes, even your retro bra. I want to get my camera, take a picture. I'd put it up on the inside of my locker."

She grinned, because it was such a sweet notion. "You're a long way from locker rooms."

"I don't know. I could go to a gym. I think I'd sign up for one if you'd be my pinup."

"Those kind of lockers are temporary."

His smile changed into something else. "And you're for keeps."

She stopped. Stopped everything, including breathing, because he hadn't meant… That would be ridiculous. Turning away, not wanting to see him wince at his mistake, she finished taking off her jeans.

When she reached behind to unfasten her bra, he touched her hands, moving them down. His mouth went to the curve of her neck, where he brushed away the awkwardness with his cool lips and warm tongue.

She let her bra slide down her arms, pool at her feet. His gentle hands cupped her, teased her nipples. She cocked her head to the side to give him all the room he wanted, and he kept up his delicious assault on the sensitive skin just below her ear.

Her eyes opened—she hadn't even realized they were closed. Now she was facing the mirror, but she couldn't see herself or Tucker clearly. They were shapes in the steam, nothing specific and real, and wasn't that perfect?

Nothing real. This was the image she'd hang on to. The one that felt like a dream. Anything else was too dangerous.

Tucker chose that moment to run his hand down her belly straight into her panties. Dreams be damned. His finger found the precise spots that would give her the most pleasure, and he played her like a Stradivarius.

Part of what made her body thrum was listening to his breathing change. Deepen. Grow harsh and insistent as she trembled. Two fingers pushed inside her, though the building pressure of his circling thumb was what got to her the most.

Standing was becoming an issue. She reached behind her and grabbed what she could. Lucky for her, it was mostly his butt. God, the thickness of the denim was un-

fair. She wanted skin…she wanted to grip him with both
hands and feel those muscles. Mark him so that later, when
they were in bed, she could run her tongue where she'd
scratched.

"Jesus," he whispered. The pumping stopped as he
pushed his hips forward, pressing his trapped erection
against her bottom. He hadn't even taken off her panties,
and she was going to come.

She ground back into him, even though it cost her the
pressure of his thumb, the steady buildup of intensity.
Didn't matter, his groan was worth it.

He bent lower again, and this time, he wasn't teasing.
Not with his fingers and not with his mouth. There were
no kisses. Just his voice. Closer than anything, almost inside her head as he whispered, "Come for me, sweetheart.
Come on. I want to feel you squeeze around my fingers.
Do it. I've got you." His warm breath clipped her ear. "Just
let go. Let go."

Every muscle strained. Then she shattered. But he was
there to catch all the pieces.

TUCKER WAS ABOUT AS HARD as he'd ever been, but there was
no way on this earth he was going to disrupt Annie's bliss.
She could barely stand, which he took full credit for, and
the bathtub was ready and waiting. He was going to massage her neck, even though there was no really comfortable
place to sit. But then there didn't seem to be much comfort
at all in his immediate future. Which was okay. He wasn't
the one who'd had to deal with that joke of a shower in her
farce of a cabin. He hadn't given up every luxury, every
piece of himself, to hide from an uncertain future.

He'd tried to think what he would have done in her situation, at least what he knew of it, and he doubted strongly

that he would have devoted himself to the care and feeding of abandoned animals.

"Oh, my God," she said, stirring as he pulled his hands from out of her panties. He'd made sure not to linger inside her after her orgasm, because she was sure to be sensitive and there was so much more of the night left. But it took a lot for him to stop petting her just below the line of her underwear.

"Are you ready to get into the tub?"

She nodded. Her arms dangled by her sides, her head lolled to the right. Even her eyes were half-lidded. "That was…"

"Yes," he said, kissing her lightly on the top of her shoulder. "Can you stand? Just for a minute. Let's get those panties off so you can get in the tub."

"Ohhh. The bath. Yes. Okay."

He waited for a sign she intended to move at all. Finally, just when he was planning how he could carry her into the tub without causing a horrible mess, she shifted her weight from him to her own two feet. "There we go."

"I'm perfectly capable of standing on my own," she said, awfully petulant for someone swaying as if she were drunk.

"I am very aware of that fact, Ms. Sheridan. You are capable of so much."

She sniffed, then smiled. "Are you getting in the tub with me?"

"Nope. That's all yours."

"But what about…" She turned around and put her hand directly over his cock.

He jerked back as if she'd burned him. "That's fine. We'll take care of that later. It's your turn to relax."

"That'll probably be gone by the time I'm done."

"It won't be gone for long, I promise."

She sighed, and he could see her returning from her orgasmic haze. With a two-handed push and a hip wiggle, her underpants dropped to the floor. "That was better than any massage I've ever had at any spa."

"I should hope so. Damn. What spas do you go to?"

"I wasn't being literal." She walked over to the tub and put her fingers in the water. The bubbles weren't as plentiful as they had been, but there were still enough. "Perfect."

"Good. I'll let you get settled, then come back to lend a hand."

She smiled as her eyes widened. "Like the one you just gave me?"

"I was thinking of a shoulder rub, but I aim to please."

She left her bath and circled her arms around his neck. "This is the best vacation ever. You're not what I expected."

"In what way did I disappoint?"

"Funny." She tipped her head back. "I mean. You're still here. You've been generous, and I don't mean just the check. Generous with yourself. Your time, your attention. I thought I'd show you paperwork, and take you for a tour. That would be that, and then we'd find out later whether Safe Haven made the grade. *You* were definitely a surprise."

"I guess we were both caught off guard. You're not who I pictured, either."

"I'm just a hermit who's found her calling."

He huffed. "Not even close."

She kissed him and there was no possibility his erection was going down a centimeter when he held her naked against him, when each kiss was better than the last.

When he finally pulled back, it was with great reluctance. "Your water's getting cold."

"There's more where that came from."

One more peck on the tip of her nose, and he moved

out of her arms. "Go relax. Enjoy. Soak until you're one big prune."

"Oh, that's so sweet…what an image." She laughed and stuck a foot in the water.

He left the bathroom, closing the door behind him. He rested there for a minute, waiting for his cock to settle down.

As soon as he checked his phone and saw that he had three voice mails, he cooled off. Too anxious to wait and listen, he checked the list of incoming numbers. None from George or Christian, only business associates. The pressure in his chest eased. It wasn't as if he was expecting the other shoe to drop at any second. He knew Annie was safe. So was his mother. No reason to think anyone, criminal or otherwise, was lurking in the shadows.

Only George knew Tucker had actually found Leanna and that they were in Montana. As far as Christian and Irene were concerned, they thought maybe Leanna had been located, no certainty there. He pondered for a moment, unable to recall if he'd told Irene he was in Montana. Shit. He couldn't remember. He had a feeling he had told her, but she obviously hadn't passed the information to Christian.

Restless, he picked up his iPad. The amount of work piling up and the panic he sensed in Darren's email was enough to put a damper on his mood under normal circumstances. Now it barely provided a distraction.

This wasn't like him. None of this. His original goal was met the moment he'd realized Annie was in fact Leanna Warner and found corroborating evidence. The next step should have been a phone call to the New York district attorney's office and a return trip home.

He hadn't even been gone that long, which made no sense. He felt as though he'd known Annie for weeks. Longer. The connection with her had been fast and deep, unlike anything he'd experienced before.

His unromantic soul had dismissed such a thing as possible. And yet here he was, having willingly put his life on hold. He'd written her a twenty-thousand-dollar personal check. That did not happen.

He'd been raised to be cautious not only with money but with his trust, his admiration, his affection. She'd broken through all his barriers with no apparent effort.

Looking at the bathroom door, imagining her soaking in the tub, eyes closed, the water lapping at her skin, he realized he wouldn't have changed a thing. Not that there wasn't more work to do, because now that he had her, he wasn't about to lose her to false identities and an overeager D.A.

The thing with Christian wouldn't be easy, though. Their relationship was already so muddled, and now with his mother pinning all her hopes for the future on winning her son back, Tucker had no idea what the outcome would be. It wouldn't do him any good to keep beating himself up for being so intentionally blind to his brother's connection to the embezzlement, but it was hard not to regret it. Not simply on his mother's behalf, either. He would like to have a brother again, not a memory overshadowed with guilt.

Now, all the blinders had to come off. He hoped there were extenuating circumstances and that Christian would walk away from this debacle with his reputation intact. Maybe he and Annie had both been duped somehow, or Christian had been the one coerced by bookies. What a mess.

His gaze fell on his briefcase, the files for Leanna Warner locked safely inside. In a way, he had known Annie longer than a few days. He'd studied her past, learned who she'd been as a teenager. How honorably she'd conducted herself as an adult. He knew her better than he did Christian. Tucker wasn't wrong about her. No doubt in his mind. The woman described in those files was exactly the one behind the bathroom door. Someone like her didn't suddenly rip off charities.

She was, however, a woman to whom he'd promised a shoulder rub, and he was nothing if not a man of his word. He put away the iPad. The real world would suck them back in soon enough.

ANNIE'S IDEA OF HEAVEN was made complete when Tucker took off his clothes. She'd even made sympathetic noises when he complained about how cold the bathtub rim tiles were on his ass as he settled himself behind her, his legs in the water on either side of her arms.

But the true beauty of this moment of perfection didn't hit until he began rubbing her neck. His technique was basic and effective. Mostly just hands on skin and pressing down on parts that hurt until they stopped hurting.

Eyes closed and body floating on a sea of endorphins, she moaned as she let him have his way. It surprised her to find she'd been running her hands up and down his legs, because she didn't remember starting. It was nice, though. He had great calf muscles.

"Oh, right there," she said, as his thumb went deep right next to her spine.

"You should get more massages."

"I should also have my meals catered by Nobu, but that's not going to happen, either."

He sighed as his magic fingers continued, sometimes gently, sometimes with true commitment. "Did you grow up in New York?"

She nodded. "Queens."

"Ah."

"Lots of trains to the city."

"Huh. Where did you develop your love of horses?"

"Books first. Then a pony at a birthday party. Don't stop."

And he didn't, until he'd worked out a particularly stubborn knot at the edge of her scapula. When he was allowed to move at his own discretion again, he said, "And after the pony?"

"Central Park. They have stables. I started working there when I was sixteen."

"Wasn't that quite a commute?"

"For a guy from Dallas, you sure do know a lot about New York."

"Practically the whole world knows about New York. But I've been there quite a few times, and the foundation works with a sanctuary in Watkins Glen. I also do business with several companies that have their headquarters in Manhattan."

"Watkins Glen. I know that place." She started to twist around but he urged her to stay facing forward. "They do a great job."

"They do."

"I worked at the stables so I could ride for free. I loved it. Loved them. I knew every inch of the bridle trail."

He rested his hands on her shoulders. "I never asked about what you did before Safe Haven. Were you working with horses?"

She stilled, the euphoria of the last hour draining away, replaced with dread. "No. No horses. Just people. Who are much more complicated." Squeezing his legs, she tilted her head up. "The water's getting cold. What do you say we get warm in the shower, then crawl into that big king bed?"

His smile assured her that her distraction technique had worked. She felt sure he hadn't been snooping outside of regular curiosity. If he tried to find her on the internet, he'd find nothing—which in this day and age was suspicious in itself. The trick was to say enough without appearing cagey. She hated that she had to hide any part of herself from him.

Thank goodness for the cold, because it let her hide her discomfort behind a fluffy towel and shivering. It wasn't until he kissed her under the hot water of the shower that she was able to really relax. And to remember who she was dealing with here.

He believed in her, and if that wasn't the most amazing thing she'd ever been told, she didn't know what else could be.

She pulled him into a wet kiss, even though it turned out not to be her best idea, then continued kissing after they'd finished coughing. His hands were all over her, exactly where she wanted them, and now it was her turn. Not in the shower, though.

After he shaved, he took over drying her hair. Dressed only in a white towel, he'd sat her down on the closed toilet and rubbed her gently but thoroughly. No man outside of a salon had ever done that for her before. There were so many firsts with Tucker.

When he was satisfied, she'd run her fingers through the damp strands, knowing she would look like a scarecrow in the morning with nothing on hand to repair the damage. Not caring in the least, she led him to the bed, both of them naked and eager.

He threw back the bedding, and they burrowed into the warmth of body heat and soft sheets.

She ran her hand all the way down his chest, lingering over a nipple, his hip bone. When she moved slightly to the right, she found his hardening penis waiting.

He gasped when she ran her finger from the base to the crown.

"You were right," she said. "It didn't take long."

He rubbed his smooth, shaved jaw over her cheek. "That's completely your fault."

"Really?"

"Absolutely. I've been in trouble since we wrestled with Pinocchio. I'm sure you know that."

"I had a hint when we were patching each other up."

"Well, sure you did. We might not have smelled great, but we had chemistry from the start."

Grasping his shaft and learning the feel of him, she looked into his eyes, enjoying the effect her grip had on him. "You were very professional. Most of the time, anyway."

"Let's not use that in the testimonials, okay?"

She laughed, gave him a squeeze and slipped under the covers, wiggling until she'd lowered herself into position.

"Oh, God," he said.

His voice was muffled, but not his enthusiasm. He grew harder as she started to stroke his shaft, slowly at first, learning, memorizing. She inhaled deeply, wanting his scent to imprint, against her better judgment.

When she finally tasted him, a lick over the silky head, she felt his body jerk and heard his low moan. Another lick, and suddenly the bedding was thrown back, and he was reaching for her with one hand, trying to find a condom on the nightstand with the other.

13

TUCKER RESENTED THE BEAUTIFUL spring morning. Resented having to get out of bed, resented that she needed to get back to Safe Haven. That he had to make his own plans to return home. While they were still in Kalispell, there was no way he'd drive them back to Safe Haven before Annie had breakfast, and more. The in-room coffee hadn't been nearly enough for her. But then, the energy boost was necessary after spectacular wake-up sex.

He shook his head, dismissing the idea that what they'd experienced was just sex. He'd had that. He knew what it felt like, and what they'd done in the past couple of days was far more. Dangerously more.

He looked through the window of the beauty shop to find Annie leaning back over the deep sink where the hairdresser was washing her hair and giving her a scalp massage. Tucker had caught her cursing at her hair this morning, preparing to wet it all over again because it evidently made her look like something from a "before" photo. So he'd gotten the name of a salon from the front desk, and while he'd had to practically hog-tie Annie to agree, she'd eventually given in. But only after swearing she'd be cranky the whole ride home.

He'd deal, although he didn't honestly believe her. She hadn't been pampered in so long. She'd never indulge herself with so much as a simple professional trim, and it gave him great pleasure to be able to step in.

It also gave him some time alone. Satisfied that Annie was all set for a while, he pressed his mother's number as he walked to the hotel's parking lot.

"Tucker. I'm so glad you called. I have to leave in fifteen minutes, but I wanted to know if there's any news."

"Good morning to you, too, Mom."

He heard her tsk. "Good morning. Now, what's happened?"

"What's happened is that you told Christian. We spoke about that."

Her pause wasn't long. "I know you asked me not to, but he was so depressed. He'd just found out he hadn't gotten that job with the insurance company. The news had brightened my day so much, I simply couldn't keep it from him. Forgive me?"

He sighed, not trying to hide his frustration. "Did you mention where I am?"

"No. I didn't think that was necessary."

So Tucker had told her. He wished he hadn't. "Good. Christian doesn't need to know. We don't want him doing anything rash. Understand?"

Her silence unnerved him. "That's not quite all my news," she said, her reluctance plain.

Tucker stopped his idle pacing. "What?"

"Even though he was thrilled that you were trying so hard on his behalf I could still hear how down he sounded. There's a long road ahead, even if it turns out you have found that woman. There's a trial and evidence and his name will be suspect for who knows how long."

That wasn't his mother's reasoning. In fact, Tucker could

hear the words coming out of Christian's mouth. "How much?"

"Enough for him to take a nice vacation and to keep him in rent for a few months."

"So, what, ten thousand? More?"

"It's my money."

Who was he to talk when he'd given Annie twice that amount. "You're right. Of course. Did he say where he was going for this vacation of his?"

"Bali. Turns out he has friends there who run a hotel. He even got a deal on the flight, so that's wonderful. I think it will do him a world of good. He'll keep in touch, though. Get all the updates."

Tucker's blood chilled at her first word. Christian had left the country. Out of fear, certainly, but of what? That uncovering Leanna's whereabouts would stir up a hornet's nest? Or that Leanna coming forward would take away his scapegoat?

He supposed his brother could be telling the truth. He could very well have friends in Bali. He hadn't been able to find a job, and to the best of Tucker's knowledge Christian hadn't traveled often.

Still, Tucker couldn't deny that knowing Bali belonged to one of the few nations that didn't have an extradition treaty with the U.S. made him nervous.

"Tucker? Are you still there?"

"I'm here, Mom. You didn't tell me where you were headed this morning."

"I'm going to Dallas, where I'm shopping with Nancy Voorman and then we're having lunch before we get our nails done."

"Glad you're getting out." He glanced at his watch. George needed to know about Bali. "So I'll see you soon."

"Soon? I hope so. Your assistant has been, shall we say, pensive about your return. And I've missed you."

"I'll be back as quickly as I can."

"I suppose that'll have to do. Bye, dear."

Tucker disconnected, then moved out of the way of a car attempting to park as he tried to gather some perspective about Christian's disappearing act. He didn't have enough information to go on, that was the problem.

His palms growing clammy, he speed-dialed George. Annie had left everything she had behind. Now, so had Christian. What the hell had they gotten involved with?

George's phone went straight to voice mail, so Tucker left a message, then headed back to the salon. Annie probably wasn't ready yet. Or maybe she was. All he really cared about was that he knew exactly where she was and that she was safe.

Nothing he'd learned had changed Tucker's opinions about her. He still believed in her. Even if she'd made a mistake, he was completely convinced that she hadn't intentionally done anything malicious or underhanded.

ANNIE TURNED TO CHECK THAT THE cooler, purchased to hold all the deli treats she'd bought, was really there. Sitting on the backseat of Tucker's rented Land Rover. It was.

She thought of pinching herself as a secondary verification, but that seemed over the top. Besides, if she'd been clever enough to dream the past twenty-four hours, she'd be smart enough to include a pinch to go with it.

Instead, she looked at Tucker, remembering the feel of his dark hair through her fingers. Lord, he had a great face. The profile was rugged and handsome enough to be on a billboard. But, as with all people she grew to know, his looks had taken a minor position in her list of reasons she'd never forget him.

She wasn't immune, and she enjoyed his attractiveness, but there was so much more to him. The salon had been his idea. She couldn't think of a man in her life who would have had that kind of insight and care. "Thank you for the beauty shop," she said. "I'm surprised it occurred to you."

"I figured it had been a while since you'd taken the time to get pampered."

"You know, you're basing your assumptions on very little real evidence."

"Ah, but I have eyewitness testimony. Your friends were impressed but concerned that you don't take much time for yourself. Besides, I'm not as dumb as I look. In some circles, I'm considered astute."

She grinned, even as the guilt over her lies threatened to overshadow her glow. The battle was tough but her time with him was so short she didn't give in. "Does that kind of talk work with the ladies in Dallas?"

He shrugged. "Used to. Not so much anymore."

"Why not?"

"The women in my life, who are mostly friends, by the way, are far more impressed with substance than flash. Although come on, you have to admit, I do have a decent sense of humor."

Mostly friends? There was a thought that was being banished right that second. Of course he had women in his life. He'd told her he hadn't found the right woman. That was still true, and she'd better not forget it.

"Are you planning on leaving right after you drop me off?" she asked.

"I should, but I haven't decided if I'm flying out tonight or tomorrow morning. Tomorrow's stretching it." He reached over and squeezed her thigh. "But I'm finding it difficult to leave."

"Oh, well, that's... Yeah. Well, you're welcome to stay as long as you like."

He smiled. "Thanks."

She laughed at herself, shaking her head. She was way too comfortable with him. It was nice. Scary, too.

"Unfortunately, my staff are becoming panicked. I don't normally take such impromptu vacations," he said. Then, before she had a chance to respond, he switched gears. "What about you? You figured out how you're going to spend the rest of the money?"

"Basics, mostly. Nothing glamorous. I'll get some plans worked up for the new quarantine barn. Maybe start laying in supplies." Her brain veered toward overload and she had to rein in her thoughts. She didn't want to give up a single minute of her time with Tucker. "Depends on how much I have to spend to fix the things that have been cobbled together with duct tape and a prayer."

"I have a feeling you'll be getting more funds relatively soon."

"I thought you said that's not your decision."

"It's not. But I know what the foundation criteria are because I helped write them. Unless there's a compelling argument against Safe Haven, which I can't imagine happening, I'm confident the board will vote in your favor."

"That would be great. Wow. Better than great."

"You'll have enough to turn that mouse hole you're living in into a storage shed. Build yourself something with a bit more breathing room."

She turned to face the road ahead, leaving the subject with a quick nod. "Safe Haven, for all its trouble, is perfect for me. I'm busy all the time. I go to bed exhausted and wake up ready to go at it again. It suits me."

He touched her hand. "The work is too demanding

to come home to that tiny place. If for nothing else, you should have a decent bathtub."

She turned her hand over and threaded their fingers together. All she wanted to do was tell him the truth. Right now. Everything. Her mistakes, her naivety, how she'd gotten caught up in a lifestyle that didn't belong to her. That she'd run as much in shame as fear, and how each day compounded the pain she'd caused her family, her friends.

It wasn't the fear of losing him that stopped her, even though she was certain she would. It was losing the best chance Safe Haven had to become what the sanctuary could be. Not only a place to save so many animals, but to teach and train the next generation of caretakers.

While her life might have turned into a sordid melodrama, her legacy could still be worth something. Even though no one from her other life would know. She would. That counted for a lot. Made waking up each day a bit easier.

"You okay?" he asked.

"Fine. Sorry to see the interlude end." Squeezing his hand, she said, "I don't want to get all sappy or anything, but, well, you've been the best part of—" Her voice broke. She cleared her throat, then whispered. "Just, the best part."

PULLING INTO THE PARKING LOT at Safe Haven was bittersweet at best. Tucker got out to carry the food chest into the cabin so that Annie could decide which small items she could fit in her fridge.

Before he'd even shut the back of the Land Rover, Shea spirited Annie away, and not in the direction of the cabin. She'd given him an apologetic smile before she'd let herself be taken, anxious to find out what had gone on during her absence. It alarmed him, but Shea didn't seem off. Though with her it was sometimes hard to tell.

Jesse showed up. "Everything's fine," he said, walking with Tucker. "Doc Yardley came by and gave all the mares and foals a clean bill of health. But I suppose the ladies want to chat."

They entered the matchbox house, his mind still struggling to accept the fact that someone lived there full-time. Annie lived there. Mostly on her own. What in the hell were her winters like? They were so far up north, the snow had to be brutal. He knew the statistics about volunteers in winter. People meant well, but putting out feed during a blizzard was nobody's idea of fun. Especially when it could so easily be seen as someone else's problem.

The idea that Annie could get hurt alone in the middle of nowhere made him feel ill. He put down the ice chest and excused himself, shutting the door to the small bathroom behind him—he had to make a phone call, and it was the only remotely private place to do so.

The Annie situation had grown exponentially. It had a lot to do with the sex, of course. The intimacy between them had been as easy as taking the next breath. He wanted her all the time, his need becoming like a persistent low fever. He'd managed to wait patiently in line at the deli for her to pick out her food, and he'd only kissed her when he was sure she wouldn't be embarrassed. But dammit, the memories of their night together made it hard to think straight.

He didn't want to leave.

He had to leave.

The sooner, the better. Where the hell was George, anyway? On top of everything else, Tucker was getting worried about his friend. He was no spring chicken, although Tucker would never say that to his face. George was about ten years younger than Tucker's father...his adopted father. He'd been a police officer in Brooklyn for years, worked vice and homicide, and he'd gotten more than a few commendations. But he'd hated the bureaucratic red tape, quit the force and got his private investigator's license.

He'd met Michael Brennan during a bar fight. Neither man had meant to be in that particular bar. Just passing the time in what normally was a quiet place in Manhattan. The fight had nothing to do with them, but together they'd stopped it, not without injury. Nothing that a couple of cold ones hadn't fixed, though.

They'd stayed friends till the end of Michael's life. George had helped carry the casket. If something happened to George because of this investigation, Tucker would find it difficult to forgive himself.

He dialed the man's number again, only to have it go straight to voice mail. He left a message that was as succinct as he could make it. Seconds after he'd hung up, he heard the front door close.

Of course, Jesse had heard him. You could hear a mouse fart from upstairs in this place. At least Tucker hadn't said anything that would get him in trouble.

Leaving the bathroom, he stayed put and didn't go looking for Annie. He supposed in a few minutes he'd find Jesse, do the polite thing and socialize, but for now, he needed to sort out a few things.

First, a flight plan. He had the number for the Kalispell city airport in his wallet, and he called in for an 8:00 p.m. departure. That would give him five more hours with Annie. Which wasn't enough time, not by a long shot.

More of an issue was how in hell was he going to tell her that he was Christian's brother? Not this afternoon. Too soon, not enough information. He wasn't ready. He was scared out of his friggin' mind that she'd hate him.

He tried to imagine her reaction to his explanation, but he couldn't get past the look of certain betrayal he'd see in her beautiful blue eyes. Even if she listened to everything he had to say, she could have her own reasons for not wanting to face what she'd left behind. He wouldn't presume to tell her what she should do. A night of sex didn't give him any rights.

Except it hadn't just been sex, and that was the problem. Damn, he couldn't remember the last time he'd felt this powerless. Or this infatuated with a woman.

The cabin door opened, and Jesse stuck his head in. "Am I interrupting?"

"Nope. I'm done making belligerent phone calls."

"No problem. I'm here on a mission." Jesse snorted. "I have to get the matzo ball soup out of the cooler, put it in the dark blue bowl and leave it in the microwave."

Tucker had to laugh. "That's a pretty serious assignment you have there, son. I was there when she ordered that soup. Messing up would not be wise."

"Thanks for the heads-up."

Tucker knew which container held the soup, so he brought it out.

"I gotta say..." Jesse found the specified bowl. "That check you wrote for Safe Haven was a hell of a gesture."

"I consider it a great investment."

Jesse's faint grin spoke loudly.

"Yes, it's because of Annie." Tucker only felt defensive because he was already edgy. "She's doing an excellent job here."

"No one said you can't have more than one reason for doing something."

"Yeah, well, I suppose I asked for that." Lack of sleep was getting to him. "By taking her to Kalispell overnight. Hope that doesn't give her grief."

"Sadie will take care of any gossip."

Tucker liked Jesse and his unhurried, easygoing manner.

"I'm concerned about the winters here. Annie being alone. You have some kind of system set up to check on her?"

"Glad you asked," Jesse said, closing the microwave. "My brothers, me and several other nearby ranchers keep in touch. When it's bad, we come in shifts, so we can all take care of our own stock. It kind of depends on how many animals Annie has here. We haven't had to rescue her yet, though. She keeps up on the snow maintenance, so she has clear paths. That's one reason we need that tractor fixed. It doubles as her snowplow in winter, and we can't let her be without that."

"I've been dealing with the drought so long, I haven't given much thought to severe winter conditions. I'm glad to hear you all are pitching in."

"Winter's tricky. I'm able to fly most days. Sometimes we'll get stuck in a cycle that shuts everything down, but the airports are well maintained. If you ever want to fly back, give me a call. I'll let you know the conditions, give you the coordinates for the private airfield I use. I checked it out already. You're welcome there anytime."

Tucker leaned back against the counter. "I'll be sure and take your number. Thank you."

"She's the real McCoy, you know," Jesse said, taking a seat on one of the wooden chairs. "My...Shea has been known to keep Annie in coffee when she needs it, and food. Annie's gone without, though. Not sure how often, but more than once."

"You don't have to sell me on her. I'm going to do what I can to get some funding for this place. Steady funding."

"Good enough." Jesse kicked out a second chair. "So tell me about your plane before the women come and monopolize us. I've been meaning to ask you about it since you arrived."

14

"I DON'T HAVE THE RIGHT WORDS," Annie said softly, watching Puff, the beautiful chocolate-brown foal, find her footing with unmanageable legs.

"You're doing pretty well," Shea answered. "To be honest, I only understand because of what's happened with me and Jesse. I had no idea that people could honestly fall in love in such a short time. I'd always thought it was fiction."

Annie jerked her head up to stare at Shea. "I'm not in love with him. I didn't say *love*."

Shea pressed her lips together as she lifted her shoulders. "Sorry. I know you didn't say the word, but the way you speak about him. I guess I was wrong."

"Really? What I said made you think...?"

Nodding, Shea met Annie's gaze with the honesty she'd come to respect. "I can't tell you what you feel. In fact, I'm terrible when it comes to reading people. But your body language changed when you were telling me about the way you two talked in the car. And you just lit up about him taking you to the salon."

"Huh." Annie thought about the past twenty minutes. After being given a rundown on Safe Haven, she'd told Shea almost everything that had happened. Not the details, of course. There'd been so much else to say. His kindness. The laughter. The way she felt connected to him. Maybe Shea was right. If things were different, Annie might have let herself think it was love. But if she went there, she didn't know if she could bear him leaving. And how could she keep her secret from someone she loved?

She crossed her arms over her chest and stared down at her boots. "I want to tell him what happened. So badly, Shea, I can hardly breathe. I hate the lies and the hiding."

"Then tell him."

"I can't. I'm a criminal. I'm working under a false name. I've lied to him from the start."

"You're not a criminal. You did nothing wrong."

Annie's head came up. "I was responsible. I was an idiot. Charities lost a lot of money because I was reckless and too trusting. How is that not doing anything wrong?"

"Okay, maybe there were mistakes, but Annie, you didn't do anything illegal. That's what matters. You didn't steal a single penny. You're not a thief."

"Just a coward and a dope."

"You're not, though. You're one of the strongest people I know. Tucker seems like a smart man. Every question he asked about the foundation was astute and reasoned, and so was every question he asked about you. Give him the benefit of the doubt."

"I believed that about my associate in New York." She led Shea out of the stable. "If it was only my feelings at stake, I would talk to him. But he's basically told me he's going to champion Safe Haven with his foundation. We have so much to lose. You know as well as I do that people can forgive a lot, but being duped, being manipulated and lied to, goes straight to their pride. Believe me. I know. Tucker's a lot of things and one of them is proud."

Stopping at the doors, she looked around, made sure

no one was nearby. "He said it himself. When he handed me the check. He believes in me. After that, how can I tell him?"

Shea sighed. She looked sad and worried. "Where does that leave the two of you?"

"Nowhere. He's going home tonight or tomorrow morning. I won't encourage him to come back."

"But—"

"That's the way it is. I'll be fine." Annie didn't quite believe that, but she hoped Shea did. "Especially now that I can talk to you. Although I promise, I won't make a pest out of myself."

"You aren't a pest. You're my friend."

Those few words meant the world to Annie, and she had to take a moment to collect herself. She'd never expected another friend, not ever. No, she couldn't have the man she wanted, but she wasn't in jail, she wasn't actively on the run and she was making a difference at Safe Haven. All in all, it was more than she deserved.

"Let's go to the barn," Shea said.

Annie sighed. "What's Pinocchio done now?"

"You were only gone overnight. No one had time to do anything too terrible."

"Ha. I've been at this long enough to know that all it takes is two minutes for everything to go crazy."

"Can I just finish with one thing?" Shea asked.

"Sure."

"Actually, two things. First, I wouldn't rule out telling Tucker, because I don't think he'd renege on his promises. Second, your hair looks really pretty."

Annie wanted to believe her. The fantasy of Tucker being all forgiving and magnanimous had been floating around at the periphery of her thoughts. But every time those thoughts became too vivid, she'd shut them down.

Despite the way she and Tucker clicked, they hadn't had enough time together for a deep relationship to form, even though it felt as if it had.

Things that sounded too good to be true, were. Not remembering that basic premise had gotten her into this mess in the first place. "Thanks," she said. "I like my hair, too."

"I MEANT FOR YOU TO MICROWAVE soup for yourself, as well," Annie said. "Why don't you have this bowl, and I'll get some more out."

"I'm fine," Tucker said. "I can have a sandwich. Or a frozen burrito."

She smiled at him as she crossed the very short distance between them. "It was nice that Shea and Jesse were able to help out. But I'm glad they're gone."

The moment she was close enough, he pulled her into his arms and kissed her. It felt risky here, as if at any moment someone from town could walk in and find them. But who would come, and why would anyone care? She supposed paranoia was her natural state now.

Regardless, it felt wonderful to press up against him, to taste him, to have another opportunity to memorize all she could before he left.

The thought that this might be the very last kiss made her desperate, and with her lips and her tongue and her breath, she selfishly took all she could, but she didn't care. It terrified her to think of him fading away in her memory. Even if she took the shirt he was wearing, kept it with her always, in time the scent would go, and she'd be left with a plain white Oxford that would torment her for the rest of her days.

Her frenzy must have been catching, because he became just as ruthless, running rough hands down her back, moving his muscled thigh between her legs. The pressure made her squirm. She leaned away, looked at the stairs.

"I made arrangements to fly out at eight."

"It's only a quarter to six," she said. "We have time. If you don't mind taking your sandwich with you."

His smile did things it shouldn't have been possible to do. "I'd never eat again if it gave me more time with you."

"Oh, that is such a horrible lie. But I'll take it."

"An exaggeration, perhaps," he said, turning her around and pointing her at the staircase. "Not by much, though."

"Eight o'clock, tonight?"

"Sadly, yes. I know that doesn't give us much time, but I'd like to…"

She ran halfway up to the loft before she laughed and said, "What? What would you like to do?" She scrambled the rest of the way up when he lunged for her. "Just know you'll have to deal with the miniature shower. Say goodbye to washing anything that requires bending over."

He reached her in record time, ducking his head just enough not to get a concussion. "Speaking of bending over."

"Hmm. Normally, innuendos don't get me hot."

He paused briefly before pulling out his wallet. "I'm supposed to say something clever now, but I can't think of anything but being inside you."

She sighed, retrieved the condom packet from his fingers and tossed it on the bed. "That was better than clever. Now, kiss me and make me forget about later."

Tucker kissed her the whole time he took off her clothes, except for the removal of her shirt and her boots. Everything fell where she stood, could have disappeared from the planet for all she cared. Besides, he had more buttons to undo, which she stumbled over, before he broke down and pulled the shirt out of his jeans.

She'd finally gotten everything undone, when he stepped back. "What?"

His scowl was fierce, but he wasn't looking at her. "What the hell is it with the boots? Why don't we wear sensible shoes that we can toe off while we're walking?"

"Loafers on horseback? I don't know, I think there'd be complaints."

"Only from people who don't have a beautiful woman who is currently naked and inches from the bed."

She giggled. God, what was wrong with her? She never giggled.

He paid attention to the task at hand, while she fussed with her comforter. She remembered the fantasies she'd had about having him between these very sheets. It hadn't dawned on her that it could be something real.

She decided to appreciate the gift, and let any other expectations go. He was here. Now. And now that his frustrating boots were off, he kicked his pants so far they caught on the railing.

He swept her up, then. Onto the bed, where they touched each other with trembling fingers and eager lips. Nothing fancy happened, and that was fine with her. Great, in fact, because she wanted him inside. Deep. She wanted to squeeze his arousal, make him remember what it felt like. Not just the wet heat, but what she sounded like when she moaned, and how her hand felt in his hair as she pulled him down to kiss her.

They rattled the headboard and banged up the back wall, and if the coyotes didn't hear them when they came, the pack must have moved to Canada.

When they found their breath again, the air was filled with their mingled scents, earthy and primal, and she almost wept that she couldn't freeze the moment, keep this as the only time instead of the last time.

THE SHOWER WAS AN ABOMINATION. Annie had been right. Bending over was a joke. He supposed it beat not having any shower, although he could argue the point.

At least he was no longer sticky. Unfortunately, he also no longer smelled like sex. That wasn't something he'd ever felt bad about before. He pulled on his clothes and avoided thinking beyond the next few minutes. They'd eat, then he'd head back to Kalispell. Damn it.

After he opened a can of soda, his cell rang. He didn't even bother taking a sip because it was George. Tucker considered calling him once they'd eaten, but he couldn't. They hadn't talked all day, not since Tucker had left him a voice mail close to noon. There was too much at stake to put this conversation on the back burner. He answered, talked long enough to tell George he'd call back in three minutes, then hung up.

Annie was up next for the shower, so that would work out well. He smiled at her, aching already from missing her. "I've got to make a phone call. I'm going to step outside, but I won't be long and then we'll eat."

She pulled him into a kiss that ended too soon. "I'll be out of the shower when you get back."

He nodded, waited for her to pick up the clothes she'd stacked on the table. Once she'd closed the bathroom door behind her, he went outside. There were no volunteers at the sanctuary this evening, and after he was gone Annie would need to do the evening chores. He'd like to do them with her. Instead, he hurried behind the stable, away from the path.

When George answered, Tucker wasted no time. "You have news?"

"Yeah, I've got news."

At the tone of his friend's voice, a lump rose in Tucker's throat. "Sounds like this is going to be painful."

"You're not wrong. Christian did leave the country."

"I know. He's on vacation." This wasn't news. He'd left that information in his voice mail for George.

"I'm pretty sure that's not why he went. I'm sorry, Tucker, but he used a false passport."

"How do you know this?"

"I had someone tailing him," George said without hesitation, though Tucker's brain was on pause. How had George had the time to have someone follow Christian? "He packed heavy enough to pay over a hundred bucks in extra fees. My associate was able to get a picture of the passport, and she said it's first rate. Had to have cost Christian five grand, at least. Especially if it came with social security card and internet traceability."

"Jesus, how much money did my mother give him?"

"That kind of passport doesn't happen in a day or two. We're talking months. Many months. He's been preparing for his departure for a while."

"Since the money for the charities disappeared?"

"Possibly." George sighed. Tucker heard the sound of a pop-top opening and wished he'd brought his drink with him.

"You got my voice mail, what, around noon? You couldn't have worked that fast putting someone on Christian and finding out all this information." Tucker put the words out there, but he already knew…. He may have been myopic about Christian, but George had clearly had his suspicions.

"No," his friend admitted. "I set up a tail yesterday after I learned of the bookies." He exhaled sharply. "I really hate this. Irene is going to fall apart, Tucker. I wish we didn't have to tell her. She could just think of him taking a vacation."

"She'll find out eventually."

"His cell phone's gone dark. If you tell the authorities, they'll search his place, but they won't find a damn thing. I know. I looked. I also called an FBI agent I know in Jersey, and he hooked me up with a local agent who really knows what he's talking about. He knew exactly which bookies I meant and has a file thick as a dictionary on the way they work. They're heavily into breaking bones, kidnapping loved ones and any other kind of blackmail they can find, but they've also been linked to at least four murders. Never been convicted. No one ever testifies against them, and they don't leave a trail."

"Is there any connection you could've overlooked between them and Leanna?"

"None. In fact, the closer I've looked at her, the more I'm convinced she didn't know a thing."

"Wait," Tucker said, his pacing kicking up dust and gravel. "Just to play devil's advocate here, let me run this by you. For a minute, let's assume everything Christian told me was accurate. He had no idea about the missing money. Then the D.A. comes after him and the only thing my brother can think is that Leanna stole the profits. There's no evidence to the contrary. Nothing points to either Leanna or Christian. He hears rumors about Leanna getting tied up with some bad guys, gets scared, makes arrangements for a passport, a quick exit.

"Time goes by, nothing happens, he figures the mob has written off the loss. He can't get work, but he doesn't really need to, not after Irene gets in touch with him. Then, out of the blue, he gets word that I've located Leanna. Which scares the crap out of him, and he blows town. Takes enough money that he can make it in Bali."

George didn't say anything for a while. When he did, it was what Tucker expected to hear. "That might have made sense if this was the first time Christian's name had come up in conjunction with gambling debts."

Tucked muttered a vicious curse. This was partly his fault. He hadn't been willing to dig deep into his brother's history. If he had, this could've ended months ago. "How bad?"

"Bad enough. Not with these particular goons, no. But there's a pattern. Something he might have picked up from his old man."

"I share a biological father with Christian, remember, and I'm not a gambling man."

"No? Sounds to me like you gambled on Leanna." George hadn't meant to be cruel, Tucker was sure, but his words stung nevertheless.

"It's sure starting to look as if I backed the right horse," he said curtly, then immediately calmed down. Getting angry wouldn't help. "If I bring her back to New York, doesn't that put her in danger? Won't these bookies know Christian split, and figure she's got to know something about the money?"

"It's possible, yeah."

Tucker opened his mouth to curse as he turned, but the sight of Annie standing at the end of the building stopped him. "I'll call you back, George," he said, his heart thudding as he disconnected.

Annie was pale as a ghost, her expression one he'd seen on victims of terrible accidents. He moved toward her, taking slow, easy steps, afraid he'd spook her. She was trembling so violently that his soda, the one he'd opened, spilled over her shaking hand.

"Annie, I can explain."

She tried to respond, at least that's what it looked like, but no words came out. Finally, she seemed to snap back to herself. "You left your drink."

"I can explain."

She shook her head, still dazed, but not in complete shock. "You don't need to."

He was close enough for her to hand him the can of soda. He took it, never looking away from her eyes, dilated far more than shadows could account for. "But I do."

"It won't make any difference." She turned, headed back from where she'd come.

He wished she'd screamed at him. Cried. Run away. But her voice had sounded dead, her stride careful. He had to stop her. Let her know that he was on her side. Make her believe him.

She didn't have to forgive him, because even when his own heart was pounding like it would burst out of his chest, the most important thing was that she understood that she might be in danger. Real danger.

That he'd put her there.

15

ANNIE WASN'T SURE SHE WAS going to make it to the cabin. Her head was spinning, and she kept thinking she would throw up, but she didn't. He knew who she was. He knew about Christian. Lies. It had all been lies. It made no sense, because they'd been in bed together. She could still taste him. She'd worked so damn hard to remember everything, branding him into her being, but every sound and scent and touch had been a lie.

Somehow she was at her truck. How much gas did she have? Enough to get to the freeway. She'd go somewhere, anywhere. There were always crap jobs that nobody else wanted. She could sleep in the truck, or maybe stay at a cheap motel. That's why she had the other driver's license. To run.

Shea would take care of Safe Haven. It would all work out, except that Annie was a fool. She was so stupid it made her step falter, and she had to put her hand on his Land Rover.

Her breath caught each time, like hiccups. Her purse was inside the cabin. Her keys. God, her money. She'd only take what she'd brought with her. Nothing from Safe Haven, never. She'd just dump out her books, put some clothes in the suitcase. Why did it have to end like this? Though, what had she thought? That it would all be a fairy tale?

Her truck was so close, but her hand was sticky with spilled soda. Her things weren't here. She'd been so hungry, and now her stomach churned.

He knew who she was. He'd known who she was before he'd arrived. Was he a policeman? FBI? Or someone Christian had sent to hurt her?

Good job on that.

Broken bones would have been kinder.

"Annie!"

She winced at his voice and willed him away. The harder she tried to push herself upright, the more her legs shook. Shea. Shea would tell everyone why she left. She'd help. She was nice. Maybe. Maybe no one was nice, ever.

"Annie, please."

Lesson learned. She'd work. She'd find someplace to sleep. She'd keep to herself. No more talking to people. No more letting anyone in.

He'd lied.

Worse than that, she'd believed him.

Something gripped her wrist, and when she jerked to look, it was his hand, not cuffs.

"Please come with me to the cabin. We need to talk."

She didn't pull her hand away. She was afraid she'd fall. "There's nothing to say."

"There's a lot to say. I'm sorry you overheard that. I was going to tell you everything, but not yet. Later. When I'd fixed things."

She looked at him and it hurt. "Who the hell are you? Who sent you? I don't know anything about the money. I never did."

"I believe you."

Her laughter came out like a bark, like bile. "Liar. You planned it. All of it. The email. Everything. Is your website made up? The foundation? Who do you work for, the D.A., the police?"

"Obviously you didn't hear the part you needed to," he said quietly, his expression blank. Unreadable. But then she fooled herself into thinking she'd ever been able to read him.

She did jerk away then, and at the second pull, he let her go. "Was it funny? Did I amuse you, or was it all in a day's work? Huh? Or maybe just cruelty for the sake of it. That actually makes sense. You slept with me. You seduced me. It wasn't enough to make me trust you. You had to go the extra mile."

Closing her eyes so tightly they ached, she held back tears through sheer force of will. "The hell with you, whoever you are."

"I know you hate me right now, I do, but dammit, there was nothing funny or cruel about any of this. I had no choice."

"What?"

"You're in hiding. Living under a false name. You disappeared from the face of the earth."

He wasn't touching her, but he leaned toward her, again, his changed expression utterly new to her. Everything until now had been underlined with confidence and strength, but now he looked anxious and frightened. Not that she dared believe him.

"Look," he said, lowering his voice, as if he were afraid of scaring her. "I'm exactly who I said I was. But I'm also Christian's brother."

"Christian Andrews?" She shook her head. No, he couldn't be. Christian said he had no family. "He's your brother?"

"Yes. We share the same biological parents, but I was raised by my mother and her second husband. He adopted me."

"Well, I see lying runs in your family. You can tell your *brother* that I have no idea what happened to the money. I didn't steal it. Oh, wait…he knows already, because the thief has to be him."

"I know," Tucker said, moving closer to her. "I know."

She took a quick breath. So what if Tucker sounded sincere? He was a good actor. He'd been fooling her for days. Except the earnestness had reached his eyes, and she couldn't look there, couldn't afford to be stupid again. "What do you know?"

"Please. Come back into the house. Let me tell you everything. You need to understand what I did. Why I had to keep certain information from you."

"Nice way of putting it."

He stood straighter, frustration clenching his jaw. "What was I supposed to do? I only found you by chance. You couldn't have made yourself look more guilty if you'd tried." Tucker sighed, then gentled his voice. "If anyone should understand that sometimes lies are unavoidable, even necessary, it's you."

She inhaled and nearly choked on the breath. "The picture. It was that stupid picture from the Sundance, wasn't it?"

He nodded. "Come inside? Please? I'm not here to hurt you. I swear. I want to help." He looked down, then shook his head before facing her again. "Whatever you think of me, you need to listen because you could be in real danger. Please, Annie. I'm begging you."

God, this was so hard and, again, she'd brought this agony on herself. Was this what the rest of her life would be like? One giant mistake after the next? Because when she looked at Tucker, she saw the same man from this morning. From last night. From the bathtub in the Hilton. His eyes were pained, his brow furrowed.

And she wanted to believe him. Again.

All the energy drained out of her. Over two years of fear, of being so careful, of loneliness and regret. She'd lived a shadow life, and when she'd finally dared go into the sun, she'd been burned.

"Fine. We'll go inside." She nervously touched her hair, which brought a memory she'd now sooner forget. "I'll tell you what you want to know, but you'll be disappointed. Whatever you or Christian were hoping to find out, I don't have it. I've got nothing."

He walked with her, his hand hovering near the small of her back before he brought it, fisted, to his side. During the short trip to the cabin, he repeated the gesture three times.

She wasn't sure if she should laugh or cry. Mostly because she had no idea what it meant. Her instinct, still, was to trust him. Maybe it was some kind of reaction to his family. She'd never been attracted to Christian, not like she was with Tucker, but she'd foolishly trusted him. Christian had been clever and a smooth talker. Though they hadn't even discussed being more than business associates.

Thank God. One was more than enough.

The cabin smelled like matzo balls and chicken soup. She wanted to throw it all out, clear the air of any traces that reminded her of their night in Kalispell. Instead, she pulled out one of the wooden chairs and sat down, her hands folded on the tabletop. "What did you come here to do?"

He got out a couple of sodas and opened the cans, putting one in front of Annie. He sat close enough to see her well, probably so he could look into her eyes and figure out when she was lying. She wouldn't tell him anything but the truth, though. She was done with the secrets and lies. They'd caused her enough pain.

"I came to see for myself if you were Leanna Warner," he said. "The website photo was a bit fuzzy, and you were turned away from the camera."

"You must have confirmed it was me five minutes in. Why didn't you call the authorities?"

He shifted in his chair, drank some soda. "You didn't make sense. I was expecting someone else, even after I realized you were the woman Christian claimed ruined his life."

She blinked at the slightly disdainful way he said his brother's name. And he'd used the word *claimed*. It was nothing for her to be pleased about.… "What does that mean?"

"I was looking for an embezzler. Someone who would steal money from charities. I thought I had managed to make some pieces fit when I took into account that you'd only skimmed the profits. What kind of thief leaves the original investments? That part was confusing before I left Dallas. Meeting you, some pieces fit. But not enough."

"Maybe because I didn't embezzle anything."

"I know that now," he said, and couldn't be more matter-of-fact. "Hell, I knew before now."

"When?"

"Did I know you weren't guilty? The first day."

She shook her head. It hadn't been a trick question, but it told her that he wasn't being entirely truthful. The first day? Did he think she was that stupid? Well, yeah, he probably did, because that's how she'd played things.

"I didn't say I thought you were innocent." His brows lifted, his gaze steady. "Not guilty is different."

Annie thought for a moment. "You believed I knew something and kept quiet."

"Actually, after I met you, my theory was that you did embezzle the money, but you were coerced."

"That's still stealing."

"Yes, but with mitigating circumstances."

She broke down and picked up the can of soda he'd brought her. Her hand still shook, but her mouth was dry and she needed the liquid. Maybe he was telling the truth. He could've given her a fluffy answer.

"Look, I've had someone working on what happened to that money. He's good at what he does, and he's thorough."

"And?"

Tucker took in a deep breath, wiped his face with his hand before he let it out. "I'll tell you everything, but first, I have to understand something. Why did you run?"

Her face filled with an all too familiar heat. More than any one thing that kept her awake at night, her skipping town was the worst of it. "I didn't even know anything was wrong until I got word I was going to be subpoenaed by the district attorney. I thought it was a joke, until I checked the accounts. All the investment interest, dividends, were gone. I'd made a client's deposit the week before, and the account had been in perfect order.

"I freaked. I had raised all the original funds and made promises about the rate of returns. So I went to an attorney, an old college friend. I told him what had happened, that I had no idea how the money had been taken or by whom."

"Did you ask Christian?"

She stared at Tucker. "Of course I did. He was more freaked out than me. He told me he was calling the Securities and Exchange Commission, the trade commission, the CEO of the brokerage. He swore he'd get to the bottom of this, no matter what."

Tucker nodded slowly. "Sorry, go on."

She drank more soda and realized she wanted water,

but she couldn't seem to move. "My attorney made some phone calls. Because I hadn't been served yet, or accused of any crime, he didn't have to report me. Anyway, he told me that the D.A.'s office was out for blood because it was charity money missing. The embezzlement had even hit the papers, although it seemed everyone's attention was on Christian. He was the most logical suspect, but they didn't have an obvious paper trail.

"There was no question I would be included in the investigation. My lawyer didn't think it would matter that I had nothing to give the D.A."

"What does that mean?"

"He said that in the end, someone would go down for the crime, and if it wasn't Christian, it would be me."

"But there was no paper trail leading to you, either."

"I had no way of knowing that. By then, I was completely shut out. Christian wasn't returning my phone calls, and when I finally did get through using a friend's cell, he hung up on me. I had no access to the computers or the accounts. It was a nightmare."

Annie stood, able to move at last. Never had she hated the size of the room more. It felt too much like a cage. "It was my own fault, though."

"Wait—"

"No, let me finish." The anger in her voice surprised her. "I'd been riding high for months, doing the best work of my life. Getting into the right parties, taking meetings with people who really mattered. I should have asked more questions, been more careful. I got cocky. When the world came crashing down around me, I had no idea who had the kind of power necessary to do the job so smoothly. I couldn't go home…I couldn't bring this kind of insanity into my parents' lives. So I bolted. I cleared out my savings and took off."

"Your parents wouldn't have helped you?"

Annie's throat tightened and she couldn't breathe for a moment as she remembered the last conversation with her mom. "Yes, they would have. And it would have killed them. I knew I was the weak link. The patsy. I assumed Christian was behind everything, and if that were true, I didn't stand a chance. He had me completely fooled from the beginning."

"They couldn't convict you with no evidence."

She looked at him. "Seriously?"

Tucker waved away his comment. "Never mind."

"Anyway, if it started looking too bad for Christian, who's to say he wouldn't have created a paper trail leading to me?" She expected more reaction from Tucker. That perhaps he would leap to his brother's defense, but no. Nothing. "It wouldn't have mattered if I was convicted or not. The key to successful fundraising is credibility and integrity. No one would hire me or work with me again after they discovered the money was taken under my watch. And frankly, I was mortified. For myself and my family. I couldn't stand the thought of seeing anyone I knew. I'd been just hungry enough that no one would ever believe I was innocent."

"And what about your family? Any contact?"

"I left them a letter, and sent a few hard-to-trace postcards. I haven't spoken to them since I walked away."

Tucker's fingers touched hers as she passed his chair, making her jump. Her face flamed again, her eyes filled with tears no amount of willpower could hold back any longer. "I screwed up everything," she said. "Every part, except for one."

Now it was her hand around his wrist. As tight as she could hold on. "No matter what happens to me, you need to promise that you won't let Safe Haven suffer. I've got the rest of the twenty thousand to return to you, and I can cancel the tractor engine. But the animals, they really need this place. It's terrible here in winter. You don't know."

"I'm not taking any money back," he said, standing to face her. "Annie, I'm not here to bring you trouble. I want to help you. We can find a way to clear your name. Together. You've done wonders here. I meant what I said about the foundation. Which is real, by the way."

She sat back down in her chair, pulling her hands away from him and into her lap. "I still don't understand. Why would you want to clear my name? What about Christian? I haven't heard a single word about him since I left."

"He's in Bali."

"Bali?"

Tucker nodded. "He left the country after he discovered I'd found you."

"What?"

"He used a fake passport."

So he knew his brother was guilty. Yet he still wanted to help her? Her pulse raced out of control. "Has he been hiding the money all this time?"

Tucker shrugged. "I don't know. The private detective has uncovered some issues with gambling. Up till the day the theft was reported, he'd done well with the investments. He would have made a number of great connections, considering your donors. It doesn't make a lot of sense for a man who was trying to build a career to decide stealing would be a better plan. Especially when you consider the amount."

Thinking back, Annie shook her head. "Wait. You said real danger. What did you mean?"

Despite the reasonable tone of Annie's voice and the fact that she wasn't shaking nearly so hard, Tucker found it physically painful not to comfort her. He wanted so much to pull her close, to kiss her, tell her not to be afraid. It killed him that he was causing her fear.

He returned to his chair, determined to tell her every detail. He explained about the bookies, repeating his conversation with George. Especially the part where nothing pointed at her complicity in the embezzlement.

"Then I should call the district attorney's office now," she said, no longer looking at him. Her gaze had lost its sharpness as she stared at the table. "No, tomorrow morning. They won't be there now. The sooner I let them know where I am, the better."

"What, no. I haven't finished."

That got her attention again. God, this had to be so difficult. She'd been living in a cave, for all intents and purposes. Making her life as small as she possibly could. He remembered every word her friends had said about her. How she dedicated herself exclusively to the sanctuary. Now he understood that every selfless act had been one of contrition. Atonement for sins she'd never committed.

He'd pulled her out into the spotlight, unprepared, lulled into feeling safe by his attention. He wished he'd done everything differently, although for the life of him, he couldn't see what he could have done instead. "These men... These bookies have been known to go after family, after associates."

"But if Christian took the money from the accounts, why didn't he use it to pay them off?"

"For all I know, he did. He's been borrowing a lot from my mother."

"A lot."

Tucker nodded. "I can't be sure, but I think it's in the hundreds of thousands. Maybe I'm wrong. God, I don't want to be right because, as it is, he's broken my mother's heart by leaving the country. She thinks he's on vacation."

"Could he be?"

Tucker's gut tightened as he stared at her. Still so trusting, so ready to believe better of Christian. "I doubt it, considering his timing and the fact that he used a fake passport. I never knew he had a gambling problem until yesterday. I didn't understand the severity of the situation until the conversation you partially overheard."

She sat with that for a while, the quiet only broken by a nicker from outside, the chirping of birds still out at the end of the day. "Even if he's still in trouble with the bookies, why would they think I would be useful to them? I've been gone for years."

"That's the point. You need to stay gone. Until we can figure out how to take care of this mess. I know for a fact the New York police have tried and failed to get at these bastards. No one will testify. They have people terrified. Until we know what made Christian run, I can't risk you like that."

"You can't risk me."

He hadn't meant to say it like that, but he wasn't about to take it back. "You're too important to me, Annie. I'll do whatever's necessary to protect you."

Her sigh wasn't one of affection or comfort. She sounded frustrated and the look she gave him was one he never hoped to see again. "You've already helped me enough."

"I never would have—"

Annie held up her hand. "Stop. I don't want to hear it. I understand you were trying to help your brother."

"That's partly true."

Her eyebrows went up.

"I hardly know Christian. But my mother has been drowning in guilt for losing him in the custody battle.

She's been trying to make up for it since my dad died. My adopted father. He's been gone eighteen months, and the only thing keeping my mom going is the chance to make amends to the boy she gave up."

"I'm reasonably sure she has something else worth living for," Annie said, the sudden gentleness in her voice making him swallow hard.

"But I'm not a mission," he said. "She's already got me in her corner."

"I'm sorry your family's screwed up. So is mine. But my mission is to keep Safe Haven safe. What are the chances these guys will find me here?"

"I don't know. But any chance is one too many."

"So why don't you just go home? Leave here, don't come back? What do you need me for?" She stared at him, her expression flat, her hands still.

He thought he saw confusion in her eyes, but he couldn't be sure. Of anything. "I couldn't bear it if something happened to you."

"I'm not your responsibility."

The hell with giving her space. He had to make her understand, so he leaned over far enough to take her hands in his. "Yes, I knew the minute I saw you that you were Leanna. But I also knew within the hour that you weren't guilty. I didn't understand any of the connections then. Only that no one would ever convince me that you had freely embezzled that money.

"I think I couldn't exonerate you completely because I didn't want to think Christian had committed the crime and blamed you. So I stayed to make sense of things. The longer I knew you, the more convinced I became that not only were you innocent, but that I had developed feelings for you. When I said I believed in you, I meant every word. I need you safe, Annie. I need you."

He'd never looked at anyone so intently in his life. And when her eyes softened, he felt he could breathe again.

"I understand," she said. "This has been painful for you. You would drop everything to save your brother, to be a hero for your mother. But it doesn't always work out that way. You have to understand that I feel the same way toward this place. If there's a chance the authorities or these bookies can find me, I have to leave. I can't risk it."

"I'll help you—"

"By doing what? I'm not willing to run any longer. That leaves me turning myself over to the district attorney."

"No, it doesn't. At least, not yet." He pulled his chair closer to her. "Let me get my attorney on this. He's a very influential man, and he can help with the D.A. His firm is based in New York, and he's got the kind of access we need. With the new information I can give him, there's a chance we can make a difference in the case against the bookies. Can you call Shea and Jesse to come back? I have to go to the hotel and check out, get my things."

Annie stared at him for a long moment, and he didn't even try to hide his anxiety, how badly he wanted her to be safe. Without a word, she got up, went to the counter to fix a pot of coffee. After she'd turned the machine on, she said, "They don't need to come back tonight. And neither do you."

He went to the counter, needing to say this face-to-face. "I'd feel a lot better if you weren't here alone while I'm gone. As for me, I know I don't need to come back. But I'd like to."

"For all I know, you're lying about everything. You could come back with a police escort."

"You don't believe that." He rubbed the back of his neck. She stared back without so much as blinking. "I'm not lying. I'm not hiding a thing. Not anymore. Not ever again."

She continued to study him, but gave him no feedback. The past couple of years had probably taught her how to do that. To push everything down. Trouble was, he'd seen the true Annie, the joy of her, the passion.

Her gaze dropped, as did her shoulders. "I suppose I have to trust someone," she said.

Tucker wanted to kiss her as badly as he'd ever wanted anything. For now, though, he made do with a simple, "Thank you."

16

LESS THAN AN HOUR LATER, Annie explained the situation to Jesse and Shea as Tucker brewed a second pot of coffee. Before they'd arrived, he'd made sandwiches and ensured Annie ate by silently pushing food in front of her until she did something about it.

Despite the seriousness of the conversation and her own disquiet, she couldn't help but find his actions thoughtful and sweet. Each kind or protective thing he did or said kept tipping her more toward his side. The lie rankled—of course it did—but it wasn't easy to keep throwing stones from her own glass house.

"I'll be just outside," he said. "I need to make a couple of calls."

"More secrets?" The words were out before she could think, but she was still hurting and she wasn't sorry she said them.

"No, Annie." He touched her shoulder, gave it a squeeze. She felt it all the way to her toes. His pull on her was stronger than she knew how to handle. It scared her as much as it comforted. "Want me to call from right here?"

She shook her head sadly. She'd agreed to trust him.

When he closed the door, she turned to her friends. Real friends. "I'm sorry."

"For what?" Jesse asked.

"Involving you. If what Tucker believes is true, someone could come looking for me."

He smiled at her with that slow McAllister grin. "They'd have to get past a whole lot of cowboys first."

Was it foolish that her heart seemed to swell in her chest? Probably.

"You should listen to Tucker," Shea said. "Let his attorney advise you."

"I don't want to be in his debt. I'll have no way of repaying him."

"You think he'd want you to worry about that?"

The way Shea looked at her made Annie pause. When her friend was being truly herself, she hid very little. The question she asked wasn't nearly as telling as the surprise in her expression. "He's not Prince Charming, Shea. We barely know each other. Whether he worries about it or not, I pay my debts."

Shea turned to Jesse, then back to Annie. "If his lawyer didn't have New York connections, I would have suggested mine. I still might. And I wouldn't take a penny from you."

Annie didn't know what to do with herself. Friends weren't this overwhelmingly wonderful. Not in her experience. Even before all of this, she'd had girlfriends. She missed her roommate from college, and Annie had been the maid of honor at her high school BFF's wedding. This was in a different league. "Thank you," she said. "But I don't get it. None of you seem to realize that I'm in this terrible situation because I was too focused on getting ahead. Why are you being so nice?"

"Your actions," Jesse said. "Everything you've done since you came to Blackfoot Falls has been admirable.

We're not just hicks with rose-colored Stetsons." He smiled, even made her lips tilt up a little. "You made some mistakes, but you've sacrificed enough, Annie. Let us help you. Let Tucker help you. He's a decent man."

"You barely know him."

Another one of those sly grins stole over Jesse's face. "But I know people who know him. Who've done business with him. I checked him out every way but Sunday before you got to Kalispell. That wasn't just about you, either. Safe Haven means a lot to Shea. To this community."

With that little nugget, Annie was officially dumbfounded. She appreciated everything being offered to her, but she wasn't about to let their generosity make up her mind for her.

Shea and Jesse assured her they didn't mind taking care of the sanctuary until things got straightened around. They'd even promised to line up more help, swearing that everyone who knew her would lend a hand.

As for what she was going to do about lawyers and district attorneys and Tucker… She had no idea. What she wanted to do was crawl into bed and pull the covers up over her head. The problem was, she wanted Tucker to be in the bed with her.

The man himself chose that moment to come back into the cabin. "I spoke to Peter, my attorney. I'll email him what I can, but the quicker I can courier the rest of my files to him, the better. I won't be long. Maybe four hours total." He looked at Shea, then Jesse. "You guys okay with that?"

"No problem," Jesse said. "I'll call the Sundance so nobody worries."

"Great." Tucker pulled his car keys out, and Annie had about enough.

She stood, her body thrumming with electricity. "Wait a minute. Just…wait. Quit making decisions for me, all of you. I'm not a damsel in distress. I need time to think. So just quit it. I need to do my evening rounds, and I'm late for that already."

"Maybe I could do your rounds with you?" Shea asked after a very awkward silence.

Annie's self-righteous anger withered, replaced by weary confusion. "Sorry. It's just… It's a lot to take in, and the last time I made a rash decision I hurt a lot of people."

Shea nodded. "So we'll talk. As long as you want."

"I've got you covered outside," Jesse said.

Tucker moved closer to her, but he didn't touch. "And I've got to leave. Please, just hang tight. We'll work things out, I promise."

Annie thought of not saying anything, letting Tucker believe what he wanted, but she couldn't. "I'll give it twenty-four hours. You know my priorities, and if we don't have more information by then, I'm going to the D.A."

He opened his mouth, but Annie's raised hand stopped him. "I know you mean well. But this is my mess." She closed the distance between them and put her hand on his chest. "Turning myself in would solve a lot of problems. You know that."

"If Christian is at the bottom of this—"

"Then the authorities will take care of it. But I can't sit back and watch you twist yourself in knots to save my hide."

"Twenty-four hours?"

She nodded.

His pursed lips told her he didn't like it. She could tell by his jaw the moment he decided not to argue with her. When he leaned down to kiss her, the touch of his lips was as wonderful as it was puzzling. The chaos she'd created kept on growing, spreading over people she cared too much

about. When Tucker pulled back it was clear he didn't want
to leave. But he let her go, then held the door for Jesse.

Annie slowly turned, meaning to get another cup of coffee. Meaning to have a heart-to-heart with Shea. What she
did instead was sit down on the nearest chair and fall apart.

TUCKER HATED LEAVING, BUT AT least Annie wouldn't be
alone. He knew nothing was going to happen to her tonight, but that didn't lessen his worry.

"I'm sorry about your brother," Jesse said, stopping near
the Land Rover.

Nodding, Tucker met Jesse's gaze, surprised at the ease
between them. It felt as if time had accelerated since he'd
arrived in Montana. "You know what's odd? Annie's become really important to me. I hate that my brother's involved in this, and God knows it's going to hurt like hell
to tell my mother, but I need to make sure nothing happens
to Annie." Exhaling, he shoved a hand through his hair. "I
don't mean to sound like an uncaring bastard. My mother's
been depressed since my father died, and of course I'll continue to be there for her.…"

"But you keep circling back to Annie?"

"Yeah. As if we'd been together for years, not days.
Listen." He looked at the cabin, then back at Jesse. "This
is going to sound nuts, and I swear there isn't anything
to make me believe she's in danger here, but if anything
should happen while I'm gone—"

"I'll take care of it," Jesse said. "Don't worry."

"It could mean getting her out of here. Maybe all the
way out. I mean, north."

"I understand. And I've got it covered. But nothing's
going to happen. Do me a favor and focus on driving, huh?
She needs you back here."

Tucker stuck out his hand and they shook. "Thank you. For everything."

"I'll see you later."

Tucker got in the SUV and took off. Carefully. It would defeat the purpose if he got himself killed in a traffic accident. Didn't mean he'd stopped thinking about Annie. Or his mother. With Annie it was about protection, with Irene it was concern. When he thought of his brother, there was only uncertainty. Why leave the seed money? Why not take everything? Unless he got into some trouble he couldn't get out of. He might have stolen the money as a Hail Mary pass. Which would mean he didn't go into the partnership with the intention of making Annie the fall guy.

The end result was the same, but it made it easier for Tucker to swallow. Christian was still Tucker's brother even though they'd been barely more than strangers for so much of their lives.

The drive passed more quickly than he'd assumed it would, and then he was on the phone, cursing under his breath because Kalispell was too small a town to have a courier at the ready. Something he would've anticipated if he wasn't so distracted by worry. He'd started to panic when he finally found someone who'd do it for triple pay. But it was still going to take longer than he'd like.

For a few moments he thought about flying it out himself, but that meant leaving Annie behind and he couldn't do that. Better to bargain with her to extend the deadline she'd imposed on him.

As he went through his files, he made a couple more calls. He'd already put a lot of the videos on a flash drive, so he completed the set, then went down to the hotel's business center. It was closed, but the manager opened it for him, and by the time he'd copied his case file, the courier had arrived.

George was doing the same thing with his files. There would be duplicates, but Tucker didn't care. The more information, the better. Though he worried there wasn't going to be enough time for his attorney to read through everything, let alone make any cogent suggestions.

When Tucker got back, he'd just have to make Annie see reason. Jesse and Shea were on his side. He'd shamelessly use them to make Annie listen if he had to. Especially since there was another issue besides the time constriction. It made sense for her to go back to Dallas with him. To wait there where he could keep an eye on her while the lawyers slugged it out.

The thought of her facing this alone made him irrational, so he'd have to watch his words. That's what happened, he supposed, when a man fell in love. Jesus. Somehow, he'd thought it would be simpler.

His laughter surprised him. None of this was funny. Especially that no matter what Annie decided, he wouldn't be able to let her go. Not that he'd force her into doing something she didn't want. He just knew walking away wasn't an option.

SHEA HAD BROUGHT A ROLL of toilet paper and a glass of water to the table. It took Annie a minute to remember she hadn't bought tissues in a while, and that made her smile, even though she was still blubbering away.

She wiped her face, though, and looked at her uncomfortable friend. "Sorry," she said, sniffling grossly. "It's been a tough day."

"I can only imagine," Shea said. "Do you need anything?"

Annie shook her head. Blew her nose. Then sniffed again. "You were right."

"About what?"

"I'm in love with him."

"Oh."

"You can't tell him," Annie said. "I can't let my feelings for him change anything."

Shea blinked at her and frowned. "It's already changed everything."

"No. It hasn't. He's just being nice. Don't you see, he's only in this because of his brother. And his mother. I can't make him choose me over them. That would be horrible. I'd never forgive myself."

"Annie—"

"I'm serious, Shea." She pulled off another bunch of paper. "It's bad enough that I've disappointed my family. Hurt my friends and ruined my own reputation. You think I want to take him down with me? I should just leave. Go find somewhere else I can hole up. Only this time, I won't make so many mistakes."

"Like having a friend who puts your picture up on the internet?"

Annie stared. "How did you know?"

"I've been thinking about it a lot. He was very clever. If he'd approached us any earlier, it would have been obvious, but he waited a while. Remember?"

"It's not your fault."

"I know. But it's not your fault, either."

Annie shook her head, frustration making her clench her fists. "People keep saying that when it's not true. I can't sit in this cell a minute longer. Walk with me?"

"Sure." Shea got up, headed for the door, then backtracked until she could grab the toilet paper. "I'll bet Jesse is almost done. Do you want to avoid him?"

"No, of course not. Thank you, by the way, for keeping my secret. It must have been difficult."

"Not so much," Shea said, closing the door behind them.

"I can't tell him anything about my classified contract work, either. But he understands."

"Of course he does."

"Just like Tucker understands your situation."

"You may be right, but that doesn't mean I should take advantage of him."

The walk got quiet except for the sound of their boots on gravel. The crunch sounded like home to Annie. How strange. Even when she'd worked at the stables in Central Park, there hadn't been gravel underfoot like this. Home used to sound like the click of high heels on a sidewalk. Of taxis and diesel engines, and the buzz of Manhattan.

"For the first six months I was away, I dreamed about New York every night."

"The city itself?"

"Mostly streets that I knew well. Restaurants. My apartment. Things happened in the dreams—mostly I was captured or chased or thrown into oncoming traffic, but the backdrop didn't feel like part of the nightmares. I missed the rhythm of the city, as if I'd had to leave my own heartbeat behind. Now, I can't imagine myself anywhere but here."

"You'd do okay in Texas."

"I'm not going to end up in Texas," Annie said, as fast as the words would tumble out of her mouth.

Shea shrugged as they neared the barn. "How do you know that?"

"Don't. I can't go there. I can't pretend that everything's going to be all right. It'll kill me if I do. I ran from a subpoena."

"You were never served."

"That's just a technicality."

"Yeah," Shea agreed, "but it's an important one. Why do you think all those process servers have to be so tricky?

Ducking a subpoena is a cliché because it's true. You weren't served. You didn't break the law."

"I don't think the district attorney's office is going to write my disappearance off so neatly."

"Maybe not. But I doubt you'll be going to jail."

"I owe restitution," Annie said quietly. It was the one thing she tried not to think about. She'd had nothing for so long, it had been easy to ignore the pull to make things right financially. She'd certainly never raise the money by working for a nonprofit.

"That's ridiculous." Shea had never used that clipped tone before.

It stopped her. "Why?"

"You need to let go of your guilt, Annie. It's going to ruin you, and you don't deserve that."

No response would adequately convey how wrong Shea was. So Annie didn't try. They walked again, and she breathed in the smell of the place she'd carved for herself. She had trouble thinking of herself as anything but Annie Sheridan. Leanna Warner was somewhere else, gone. Buried in shame. Annie couldn't help thinking it would be better for everyone if she simply rested in peace.

TUCKER SAT ACROSS from Annie, staring into her troubled gaze. Shea and Jesse had gone home. The cabin was quiet…and after the longest day Tucker could remember, all he wanted was to take Annie to bed.

"Me going to Dallas doesn't make sense. I told you, if we don't have more to go on, I'm calling the D.A." She lifted her chin. The woman could be stubborn. "It's not a debate."

"We can work together much easier if you're with me," he said.

"Together? What am I supposed to add to this collective? If I had some information that would help, I'd have done something with it. That's the point," she said. "I don't know anything."

"I'm not doubting you, but something you may have dismissed as unimportant might be a key piece of the puzzle. Let Peter look through the files. Let him question you. He might stir a memory, remind you of a moment or an offhand remark you thought nothing of at the time."

"He can call me here. I don't like the idea of leaving Safe Haven. This place is mine. I need to be here."

Tucker wanted to throw every last piece of furniture in this cracker box outside, give them some room to work with. He kept trying to think of a way to postpone his trip home. Staying would make him feel better about her safety, but the ranch and his responsibilities at home needed his attention desperately. There were a lot of people counting on him. Especially his mother. As much as he wanted to forget about the Rocking B, he couldn't. Not without a cost he wasn't willing to pay.

"I have to go," he said, taking hold of her hand. "But leaving you…"

Annie didn't respond. Time slid by as he rubbed his thumb on the back of her hand. He ached, physically. His mother could call Christian's phone anytime. When she discovered it wasn't working, she'd worry, and then what? Lie to her? He could, but that wouldn't solve anything.

He needed to give Peter time to familiarize himself with the case. To be effective. George was still sneaking in back doors to quietly get information on the bookies and that damn account number in Annie's coffee can.

He should ask her. Just spit it out, but that would make her even more suspicious, and rightly so. And hell, he hated admitting he'd gone through her things that first day. On the other hand, he'd promised to tell her everything.

There was no winning. Nothing he could do to help the people he loved.

"This is about your mother, isn't it?"

He blinked at Annie, not able to tell how much time they'd sat in silence. "Partly, yes."

"Oh, God. You're choosing me over Christian. You realize that, right?"

"No, I'm not. He made that choice for me."

Annie's face was flushed and miserable. "She won't see it that way."

"Probably not. At least, not at first. It's going to be difficult. I'm not even sure what I should do. I thought about making something up, but then if there's proof, and I believe there will be, that Christian was involved, it's going to get out. I don't want her caught unaware."

"She needs you."

He shrugged.

"Do me a favor?"

Sitting up straighter, he curbed his instinctive nod. "What's that?"

"Come to bed with me?"

That he hadn't expected. "Yes. Of course, yes."

"You go first," she said, looking at the bathroom door. "I've got to make tomorrow's coffee."

This time he did nod, afraid if he opened his mouth he'd say something foolish and make her renege. For the first time since she'd overheard him on the phone, the world felt normal. Well, almost normal. He brushed his teeth; she counted out spoons of coffee. They passed each other on the stairs, brushing fingers and sleeves. He could see how exhausted she was, and hoped they could both find sleep.

When they were finally in bed, her in a sleep shirt she'd put on downstairs, him in a T-shirt and his boxers, they didn't touch at all.

She lay on her side facing him, and he faced her. The room was shadowed with bands of moonlight. He assumed she could see him more clearly than he could see her. But that was okay. He knew enough about what she must be going through.

There was still a matter of trust between them. Trust and a pile of guilt on both their shoulders. "I'm sorry," he whispered, as much to himself as to Annie.

"What for?"

He didn't think she was being coy, not by the tone of her voice at least. "I'm not sure," he said. "I guess I wish we'd met at another time, another place. I want to make all the bad things disappear, and I can't."

Annie sat up so quickly, it startled him. She turned the bedside lamp on, then slipped out of the bed, down to her knees. Tucker almost sat up, but then he realized what she was doing. A moment later, she sat, cross-legged, on top of the comforter, holding a coffee can.

She didn't open it immediately, and moved slowly when she did. She took out the driver's license. The roll of money, and the slip of paper with the account number written on it. Her gaze didn't leave the objects, even when she set aside the can.

"This was my exit strategy," she said. "Part of it, at least." She held up the license. "This was someone my parents used to know. She was my age, but she died four years ago. I never met her. My mother was her godmother. It was a sad story, why the license was in the attic, but I didn't think my mother would mind if I borrowed it." She put it down again, as if it were something precious, a baby blanket or a beloved garment.

Then she picked up the scrap of paper. Shook her head, and grabbed the money roll in the same hand. "These go together. One is what's left of my life savings. I had more. Twice this much, basically. A little more than twice. Enough to make it into Canada, find a place to live. Enough to give me breathing room, because I'd learned how to keep my expenses down. But then my first winter, some horses got sick. I didn't have enough to feed them and get them medicine. I dipped into the other roll."

She put the money down and stared at the paper. "This is a bank account number. A safety net. From the bank in Blackfoot Falls. My payback account. It's pitiful, and I don't think I'll ever make enough to fully repay the stolen money, but I needed to do something real. Something more. So I saved some cash from being a waitress for three months before I came here. And I made some money doing day labor. Nothing much, barely enough to eat and have a place to sleep, but I put something aside, every time. It used to be in the can, along with the rolls. But I knew if the horses needed something, or the goats or the cows, that I'd use it. So I put it away in the bank. Where it would be safe and harder to put my hands on."

She pulled the red coffee can in front of her, and put her possessions back inside. "That's it. That's everything except for this place. Do you see? I have to do what's right, now. Because I didn't before."

He wanted to argue with her. Tell her she was taking things too far. But that wasn't true. This—the coffee can, the savings account, her crusade to save all the animals— it's who she was. Maybe she hadn't been that before, but she was now. This was the woman he'd fallen in love with.

He put his hand on the can, and she nodded, giving him permission to put it down by the side of the bed. Then he helped her crawl underneath the blankets, where he pulled her into his arms. When they were entwined, he breathed again. Felt right again.

And he knew he would do whatever it took to protect her. To keep her just as she was.

17

"So YOU DECIDED TO GO TO Dallas with him," Shea said, looking as if she hadn't gotten much sleep the night before. That probably had something to do with the fact that she and Jesse had arrived at six-thirty.

Annie had slept surprisingly well in Tucker's arms. In fact, all they had done was sleep. And although the day ahead frightened her to death, she felt all right. "He's put himself on the line for me," she said. "I have to give him the same courtesy."

"Have to?"

Annie smiled. "You're the slyest devil I know. No. I want to. If all the rest of this madness weren't going on, I'm pretty sure I'd be over the moon with happiness."

"People say, 'This, too, shall pass.'"

"People can be idiots. But in this case, I hope they're right. I don't want to hide anymore."

"Of course you don't." Shea nodded at the suitcase on Annie's bed. "That's all you're taking?"

"That's all I've got. I didn't leave with much to begin with, then had no place to store anything that wasn't useful."

"You should have said. I would have brought some

things for you to wear. Maybe not my clothes, because they wouldn't fit, but we could have come up with something."

"I'll be fine."

"You're right. You will be."

Annie closed the suitcase and turned to her friend. "I'm only able to do this because of you guys."

"It's everyone, Annie. We want you to be free and clear, here because you want to be. In the meantime, I've got Melanie and Levi and Kathy to help out. And Will, of course. Then there's all of them from the Sundance, and Matt's volunteered a bunch of manpower from the Lone Wolf. So don't fret. We've got it covered, no matter what."

"Just know that I appreciate it deeply. That I'd hug you so hard if we were huggers."

Shea laughed. "You are a good friend."

"Hey," Tucker called up the stairs. "You need my help?"

"Nope," Annie called back. "Fair warning, though. If there's no more coffee, you guys are toast." She picked up her suitcase and looked around the room, hoping like hell she'd see it, and the people of Blackfoot Falls, again.

DURING THE DRIVE AND ALL through the flight, they talked about school and sports and old friends and lovers. Family, too, but only about the past. Nothing about what they were facing. And they touched. A lot. After they landed in Dallas, he pointed out landmarks on the drive to his downtown condo, but she barely looked out the window, preferring to watch him.

"I'll give you a quick tour," Tucker said when they arrived, putting his Stetson on a peg by the door. It was the only overt sign that a rancher lived in his gorgeous seventh-floor condo. The motif was black and white with startling splashes of color and an ebony stone floor. It was so spacious that she could completely walk around every piece of furniture.

She lingered over the stunning view, then admired all three bedrooms and the big kitchen. It didn't hurt that he had a whirlpool tub that could comfortably hold them both.

Annie felt suspended between worlds. She'd never been to Texas, and already it felt foreign. The accents were strong, the humidity reminiscent of summertime on the east coast, but the air was different. Neiman Marcus was a hell of a lot bigger and ritzier than Abe's Variety, and while she appreciated the luxury and flash of the city, it was intimidating, as well. Dallas was a long way from the Canadian border.

Despite the lack of Western decor, Tucker belonged there. He eased her nerves with a cold beer and then made a quick call to a nearby Chinese place. She had to admit, takeout was something she'd missed a lot.

When they were unpacked in the master suite and seated at the dining room table, the reason for her visit came to roost. Made it kind of hard to enjoy the dumplings and Peking duck.

"I'll call Peter, as promised," Tucker said, "but I'm not expecting miracles. He's barely had a chance to make it through the paperwork."

She nodded. "When are you going to your ranch?"

"That depends on you. I'd like to go in the morning. It's not going to be an easy conversation, and I don't want to rush it."

"Okay, that's fair. I'll wait, then, to make my decision. But I have to warn you, as much as I appreciate your situation, I'm still having trouble seeing any other solution."

He inhaled, ready to give a speech that he clearly cut off before the first word. Several seconds passed before he began again. "You know what I know," he said. "I've already made sure that the plane is being serviced and refueled. If you want to go to New York as early as tomorrow evening, that's fine. I won't try to persuade you any more than I already have. Except for one last thing…"

She nodded, equally afraid that he'd change her mind and that he wouldn't.

Tucker put his hand on hers, and she rested her chopsticks on her plate, giving him her complete attention. "Somewhere in that mix of what you need to do," he said, "and what you want to do, and how you think this needs to play out, please consider the undeniable fact that I've fallen in love with you."

The rug swooped out from under her. Her few sips of beer seemed to have made her drunk, and she forgot, while his eyes peered into her own, that she could breathe.

A moment later, the earth turned as if it had never stopped. "Oh, Tucker," her voice shaky. "That was below the belt."

"I know. That's why I said it. I want you with me, Annie. Somehow. I don't know what it can look like yet—there's too much chaff to find the wheat—but I won't let this end without a fight. I love you."

"You can't." She adamantly shook her head. "You don't know me well enough." Of course she'd already admitted to herself and Shea that she'd gone ahead and fallen for him. But that was different. She saw so clearly the kind of man Tucker was. What woman wouldn't fall for him? He was loyal, thoughtful, smart, great looking.…

God, what was she doing here with him. No, what was he doing with *her?*

"Annie?"

"What?"

"Stop thinking so hard." He smiled when she sniffed. "Look, I have something else I need to come clean about," he said, and the fear edged back inside her. "I know you better than you think I do. The files on the embezzlement and your background that I sent to Peter? They're very comprehensive." He looked closely at her, waited while she processed what he was saying. "That's part of the reason I knew right away you weren't the woman Christian described."

"How much exactly did that private detective dig up?" She tried to remember if there was anything major in her past she should be embarrassed about.

Tucker smiled, and supporting his claim that he did know her, he said, "Don't worry. I wasn't privy to anything that would make you blush."

Annie laughed a little. "Yes, it crossed my mind."

He looked serious again. "Those files told me everything I needed to conclude you weren't a thief. You're that same woman, even after all the crap flung at you. I love you. Not just because you've changed your world to make things right in every way you could, but because I can see the strength in you. You've been forged in fire, that's for damn sure. It's made you sharp and extraordinary, and still somehow so kind."

He touched her cheek, a gentle sweep of fingers. "You're an amazing woman caught in a terrible web. Don't let it swallow you. Please. You've paid your penance."

Annie blinked back the tears only he seemed to wring out of her. "I'd hate to play poker with you. You're a ruthless man. But the truth is, I think I love you back."

His smile made her giddy inside. "You think?"

"Shea and Jesse fell in love in a week," she murmured, more for her own benefit than his.

"It happens. Not often, but it does." His calm self-assurance comforted her. Tucker wouldn't tell a woman he loved her if he had even the slightest doubt.

"It's been crazy. The past few days…life in general. I can't keep up with anything."

His steady gaze lit with a flicker of humor. "And yet some things remain consistent. For example, did you know that Chinese food heats up in a microwave, good as new?"

"Does it?"

He nodded. Rose. Offered her his hand.

Near midnight, they finally ate their reheated dinner in bed, with *Letterman* in the background. Worn out, they touched from hip to toes. All Annie could think was how incredibly lucky she was.

WHEN TUCKER ENTERED THE HOUSE, his mother was waiting in the foyer. She looked her elegant self, but he was reasonably sure she'd tried calling Christian and was concerned.

She hugged him, smiled, searched his face. "You look tired."

"It's been a long trip."

They walked to the staircase, where Tucker left his briefcase, laptop and hat, then went to the kitchen. It was just ten, and he'd skipped breakfast, knowing Irene would want him to eat with her. Leaving Annie behind had been hard, but she'd assured him she needed the time alone.

"You realize," his mother said, after they both had cups of coffee, "that you haven't told me if you found her."

Tucker looked at the spread on the table, all set out and waiting. A fresh fruit salad, all the fixings for the waffles he deduced the housekeeper had put in the oven to keep warm. Most likely next to the crisp bacon. "Let's eat," he said. "I'm starving, and it's a long story."

Irene went to the stove and pulled out the platters. He found the pitcher of orange juice in the fridge. They fixed their plates as he tried for the hundredth time to come up with an opening line that wouldn't upset her further.

Finally, after a few bites and verifying that Martha was upstairs changing linen and wouldn't overhear, he put his hand over his mother's. He hadn't realized, until Annie, that he only did that for two women. "I did find her. She was in Montana running a large-animal sanctuary."

Irene slipped her hand out of his grasp. "It took you all that time to recognize her?"

"No," he said. "It took me all that time to figure out what's been going on. I started out looking for the woman. When I got there, I knew I had to search for the truth."

Tears came to his mother's eyes. Of course she knew. Not the details, he'd have to give her those in painful doses, but Irene was an intuitive woman. Bali had likely tipped her off. "He'll never come back, will he?"

"I don't know."

"I'd hoped," she said, using the linen napkin to dab at her tears. "I wanted so much for this to be someone else's fault. But I left him with Rory, and for all that I'd once loved the man, he had his demons."

"Mom, please. You did the best you could. There's a time in every person's life where they have to stop blaming their upbringing or the circumstances and take responsibility for their actions. Christian's a grown man. He knows right from wrong. This isn't about you."

She tried to smile at him. "I'm his mother, sweetheart. I'll always be his mother. And he'll always be the child I left behind."

ANNIE HAD TAKEN A BATH, but the jetted water and the space to relax hadn't helped at all. Her thoughts were going in circles. For every argument to wait for the attorney to come up with a plan, there was a counterargument for her to cut through what would be an unknowable amount of time and take matters into her own hands.

She'd found a leather club chair that fit perfectly when she curled her legs under her, and sipped yet more coffee. The chair faced the big window in the living room, and the panorama of city life spread out before her seemed more like an art exhibit than reality.

It was odd to be alone. How had Tucker become a familiar and comforting presence in such a short time? That she missed him so much surprised and frightened her. Between each chain of thoughts about Christian and the bookies and the law were gaps filled with only one thought on a continuous loop—Tucker loved her.

That was the most astonishing thing of all. It outweighed all the fear and doubt and self-recrimination, and every time she started to think she didn't deserve him, his voice came to scold her. He was a smart man who knew his own mind. And he knew exactly who she was. All of it. All the things she'd hidden for so long.

Then she'd get back on the cycle of doubt and peddle that sucker until she ran out of steam.

In the end, the deciding factor came down to the fact that he loved her. Ironic, but that was the swing vote. Or perhaps, that she loved him. Either way, she knew what she had to do. For her, for him. For them.

She pulled out her cell, and called the number she'd looked up two years ago but never used.

TUCKER'S EVERY INSTINCT rebelled at what was happening. Ever since Annie had told him her decision to go directly to the district attorney and offer herself up as a bargaining chip, he'd had to work harder than ever to keep in mind that Annie was her own person. And she had a right to do something he considered unbelievably reckless. That was the trap he couldn't seem to escape. He, the man who would take a bullet for her, wasn't the one in control.

And now she was the centerpiece in a sting operation to blackmail the two bookies. Money in exchange for her silence. She'd give them recordings they believed Christian had made, then disappear forever this time. That's how it was supposed to work.

He'd just spent the most nerve-racking three days of his life. And Annie? Jesus, she was a rock.

"You're going to be surrounded by our people, Annie. Remember that," the FBI special agent told her.

Tucker knew Doreen Wellman believed what she said. Which didn't make it true.

Everyone else—Peter, the assistant D.A. in charge of organized crime, the supervisory special agent who ran the task force trying to nail Dave Bell and Mickey O'Brien, the bookies who'd been running roughshod across New York for over fifteen years—had cleared the room while Agent Wellman checked the wires in Annie's clothes.

It was something new, nothing like what he'd seen in the movies. This wire was literally the size of a fiber-optic strand, so slender it was sewn into Annie's bra, virtually invisible. Also untraceable by any technology out there. Or so Tucker had been told.

He wanted to sit back and let events unfold, focus on being supportive, but for Christ's sake, Annie was walking into a viper's nest.

As Annie lowered her T-shirt, Agent Wellman leaned back against the desk in the meeting room they'd taken over. "You did great on the phone call," she said. "You shocked Bell when you said Christian told you what happened to Jefferson Hope. Very few people knew they'd put a hit on their own bagman."

"If you have evidence, why not take them into custody?" Tucker had promised himself he'd keep his mouth shut. Tough. "Why Annie?"

"Because we can't use the recording of Annie's phone call in court. These guys are tricky and they've run us in circles. I'm not too proud to say that Annie stepping up now is a godsend. We need to get at least one of them to speak. We've fed Annie specific questions to ask them." She smiled at Annie. "You want to reassure your friend that you know what to say?"

Friend? The word was like a slap to Tucker. They were so much more. He saw in Annie's eyes that she was thinking the same thing.

She gave him a serene smile. "I warned them on the phone that I have a duplicate set of flash drives in a safe deposit box, and that if anything happens to me, the information will go directly to the police. I'll remind them as soon as I walk in. They know I've disappeared once and think I only came back because I'm broke. It's perfect, really."

"Believe me." Agent Wellman nodded her dark head with confidence. "They'd rather pay the blackmail than take a chance on their empire crumbling."

Screw her authoritative blue suit and her sensible black shoes and her calm demeanor. Tucker was sweating. And he had a few things to say about the "perfect, really" remark. Later. "Unless they decide she's bluffing and kill her when she walks in the door."

"If one of them lifts a weapon we'll shoot him. We have the best snipers in the country armed with infrared scopes at all windows. It doesn't matter that the drapes are closed. Right this second, we're watching them move around that old house. In fact, according to the man who's in a van a few blocks away, Mickey just went to the toilet. To pee."

Annie captured his gaze. "I can't give these people any more of my life," she said. "Neither can you. I heard Bell's doubt on the phone. I can't believe someone could be that good an actor with no warning. He was worried about what

I might have on them. He wanted more information, and I've memorized everything I'm supposed to say. I'll be out of there in the blink of an eye, and we'll be long gone before the world caves in on those bastards. It's going to be fine."

"I won't stop worrying until we're out of New York, and they're in jail. But I can't help asking one more time. Please don't do this. There has to be another way."

Annie leaned in for a kiss, and when she pulled back, her relaxed expression made him ache.

"I know you think you're doing this for all of us." He touched her hair. "But nothing is worth you getting hurt."

"I won't be hurt. When it's over, I'll have immunity. I'll be free, for the first time in over two years. And it'll open the door for Christian to come home."

"To jail."

"That's true, but at least it'll probably be at a country club prison in Dallas. For so little time, it'll give your mother a chance to get to know him before it's too late. Give you a chance, too."

"There's nothing I can do to get you to change your mind?"

She shook her head. "Just be waiting for me when I'm finished, okay?"

"I wouldn't be anywhere else."

Unfortunately, being where he'd promised turned out to be unimaginable torture. He'd suspected it would be, but waiting in the van three blocks away, putting on the headphones that let him listen to what was happening, only to pull the damn things off...and then repeating the cycle until he'd nearly ripped an ear off, was almost unbearable. It was all he could do not to run out of the friggin' van, get to her and take her away.

But that wouldn't happen. They'd reached the point of

no return, where anything he might do would put her in even more danger.

There was no doubt in his mind that if his prick of a brother ever came back to the States, Tucker would punch his lights out. How dare he put Annie in this kind of danger.

How dare Tucker let her go.

He moaned, and Agent Wellman brushed his arm in sympathy. She had no idea. None. They were all about the case, the people in the van and on the nearby rooftops of this rough neighborhood. Practically every person on the street was an undercover agent. There was more firepower on this residential street than at FBI headquarters. Or so he'd been assured.

Yes, he knew it was an exaggeration, and even though he'd wanted to deck the person who said it, he'd held his fist close to his body. Although he dared anyone to make one smart remark. He wished someone would.

He stopped breathing the second the door opened, and he could have sworn he didn't start again for the next ten minutes. He barely moved, didn't blink, thought he was going to be sick, or at the very least have a heart attack.

Annie was amazing. She played her part as if she'd rehearsed her whole life. The two men were disgusting, which wasn't a shock…that Tucker managed to not rip a seat out of the van was.

Every minute felt like an hour. Nothing had ever frightened him so deeply. He wasn't even allowed to see her, only hear her when she climbed into the back of a taxi that wasn't really a taxi.

He shook on the way back to Times Square, where Annie left the cab. She walked to a small hotel almost hidden by a huge marquee, and went up to her room.

He had to wait until the FBI was certain she hadn't been

followed. Thankfully, they'd detected no wires or bugs or worse in the bag that held the cash.

Finally, when he was about to burst out of his own skin, he was allowed into the room with her. He slammed the door behind him, locked it, bolted it, dragged Annie straight into the tiny bathroom, locked that.

Then he kissed her. Held her so tightly she almost choked, but then she laughed until he kissed her again. And again.

It took a long time for his heart to stop pounding as if it wanted to jump out of his chest.

Epilogue

Two months later...

IT WAS AMAZING TO MAKE the turn to Safe Haven. Annie was
smiling like a kid, leaning forward as if she'd never seen
the long dusty road.

Tucker laughed at her, but he was grinning pretty hard,
himself. "You okay?"

"I think so. It feels like coming home."

"It is. But I'm hoping that it won't take you too long to
feel that way about the Rocking B."

"It's an adjustment, I'll admit." She grabbed his hand as
the first corral came into view. "A wonderful adjustment."

By the time they made it to the parking area, she could
see the construction going on. The quarantine stable was
framed, and some of the walls were up. They weren't quite
as far on the new cabin, but that construction was fancier.
It would be a real house, with three bedrooms and two and
a half baths. Whoever ended up taking over Safe Haven
for good would be happy there. She knew, because she'd
seen every stage of the design.

Tucker's foundation had come through like champi-
ons. They'd hired quite a few people from Blackfoot Falls,

which was fantastic for the economy, and they hadn't had to turn away nearly as many horses.

Annie couldn't wait to see Shea, who had temporarily taken over the reins but shared responsibility for decision making and managing volunteers with Melanie.

"Maybe tomorrow, when we're not so tired, we can go for a ride, check out the newly plowed field."

"Yes, absolutely. Tucker, this is so amazing."

"It's always going to be yours, you know," he said, pulling the rented truck into the expanded parking area. She jumped out before he had a chance to undo his seat belt, but she waited for him before she raced to the stable.

Sure enough, that's where she found Shea. Annie almost pulled her into a hug, but then she remembered they weren't huggers. Shea just shook her head and followed through. Somehow, Annie wasn't surprised when her friend and Tucker shook hands.

"So much is happening," Annie said, trembling with excitement.

"A lot of construction. We're sending the pregnant mares to the Sundance for the time being. Too much noise."

"How are you doing, Shea?" Tucker asked. "Is Safe Haven keeping you too busy? You know I can hire someone to come out here full-time."

"I'm fine, but I was hoping we'd take a look at hiring Kathy and Levi. I think they'd like the work, and could use the money."

Annie grinned. "That's a wonderful idea."

"Now what's all this about you starting a Safe Haven in Dallas?" It was Melanie.

Annie and Tucker turned to find her taking off her gloves as she walked into the stable.

"Yep. Tucker's dedicated two hundred acres of Rocking B land for the new sanctuary. We're designing it from the ground up. It'll be a teaching facility, as well. Just like here."

Melanie gave her hand a squeeze. "We miss you."

"I know. I miss you guys, too."

"We're not leaving the planet," Tucker said. "I do have a plane."

"Can it hold a horse?"

"No. But I'm going to build a landing strip on the edge of the property so that we can start an animal rescue co-op in central Texas."

"How long are you staying?" Shea asked.

"Just a couple of days." Annie pulled Tucker closer, and relaxed as his arm went around her waist.

"We're going to visit Annie's folks for a bit."

"You haven't seen them yet?"

He shook his head. "We did. But things were more unsettled then. They need a chance to get reacquainted."

"And to give him a proper third degree," Annie said.

"Well, as long as we have a couple of days with you, why don't you two saddle up and come see what's what?" Shea asked. "Nothing like seeing your dollars at work with your own two eyes, right, Tucker?"

He looked at Annie. She knew he was beat and so was she. They'd really intended to rest when they arrived. She shrugged. "I guess I'm not capable of saying no when I'm here. You can go on inside if you like, and we can ride again tomorrow."

"Oh, no," he said. "We'll sleep in New Jersey."

She kissed him, right in front of Shea and Melanie and all the horses in the stable. "Don't count on it."

* * * * *

Waking Up To You

Gently pushing her, Oliver ordered, "Go."

All because he needed *her* to be the one who walked away
and ended this before it really began? As if he had no free will?
As if unless she did, he wouldn't be able to stop himself from
doing to her exactly what she'd practically dared him to do?

*You don't want him to do it, either, remember? You know you
can't do this.*

No. She might want Oliver, and having sex with him might
even be worth what she would go through afterward if people
found out. But she needed to cool this, here and now. She had
to be the one who walked away.

Which still wasn't going to be easy.

"I'm telling you, you really don't want to watch me walking
up those stairs."

"Yes. I really do."

"You'll regret it."

"Hell, I already regret it," he said, tunneling both his hands
through his hair this time, leaving it more tousled than before.

"Not as much as you're about to."

Without another word, she spun around again, squared her shoulders, stiffened her spine and ascended the stairs. He stood below, watching her, and when she reached the fourth one, she couldn't help pausing to glance over her shoulder at him.

"Oh, Oliver, do you want to know why I didn't want to walk up the stairs until you left?"

He didn't reply, just gave her an inscrutable look.

She told him anyway. "Because of this."

Candace took another step, knowing she'd reached the point of no return. Knowing full well he could now see what she was *not* wearing beneath her robe.

She wished she could say his strangled, guttural cry of helpless frustration made her feel better about walking away from what she sensed could be the best sex of her life.

But she just couldn't.

Pick up WAKING UP TO YOU by Leslie Kelly, available April 23 wherever you buy Harlequin Blaze books.

As a special treat to you, you will also find Leslie's classic story *Overexposed* in the same volume. That's 2 great books for 1 great price!

REQUEST YOUR FREE BOOKS!
2 FREE NOVELS PLUS 2 FREE GIFTS!

✦ HARLEQUIN®

Blaze®

red-hot reads!

YES! Please send me 2 FREE Harlequin® Blaze™ novels and my 2 FREE gifts (gifts are worth about $10). After receiving them, if I don't wish to receive any more books, I can return the shipping statement marked "cancel." If I don't cancel, I will receive 4 brand-new novels every month and be billed just $4.49 per book in the U.S. or $4.96 per book in Canada. That's a savings of at least 14% off the cover price. It's quite a bargain. Shipping and handling is just 50¢ per book in the U.S. and 75¢ per book in Canada.* I understand that accepting the 2 free books and gifts places me under no obligation to buy anything. I can always return a shipment and cancel at any time. Even if I never buy another book, the two free books and gifts are mine to keep forever.

150/350 HDN FV42

Name	(PLEASE PRINT)

Address	Apt. #

City	State/Prov.	Zip/Postal Code

Signature (if under 18, a parent or guardian must sign)

Mail to the **Harlequin® Reader Service:**
IN U.S.A.: P.O. Box 1867, Buffalo, NY 14240-1867
IN CANADA: P.O. Box 609, Fort Erie, Ontario L2A 5X3

Want to try two free books from another line?
Call 1-800-873-8635 or visit www.ReaderService.com.

* Terms and prices subject to change without notice. Prices do not include applicable taxes. Sales tax applicable in N.Y. Canadian residents will be charged applicable taxes. Offer not valid in Quebec. This offer is limited to one order per household. Not valid for current subscribers to Harlequin Blaze books. All orders subject to credit approval. Credit or debit balances in a customer's account(s) may be offset by any other outstanding balance owed by or to the customer. Please allow 4 to 6 weeks for delivery. Offer available while quantities last.

Your Privacy—The Harlequin® Reader Service is committed to protecting your privacy. Our Privacy Policy is available online at www.ReaderService.com or upon request from the Harlequin Reader Service.

We make a portion of our mailing list available to reputable third parties that offer products we believe may interest you. If you prefer that we not exchange your name with third parties, or if you wish to clarify or modify your communication preferences, please visit us at www.ReaderService.com/consumerschoice or write to us at Harlequin Reader Service Preference Service, P.O. Box 9062, Buffalo, NY 14269. Include your complete name and address.

Double your reading pleasure with Harlequin Blaze!

As a special treat to you, all Harlequin Blaze books in May will include a new story, plus a classic story by the same author, including...

Joanne Rock

As a financial researcher at a successful firm, I'm all about professionalism. As feature pole dancer "Natalie Night," I come alive and I'm irresistible. My alter ego has just opened the door to the one man who was totally off-limits. The man whose eyes tell me how badly he wants me. And the one man who can never know who I *really* am...

Pick up *My Double Life* by *Joanne Rock*

and also enjoy her classic story ***Wild and Wicked*** in the same volume!

AVAILABLE APRIL 23
wherever you buy Harlequin Blaze books.

Red-Hot Reads

www.Harlequin.com

Love the Harlequin book you just read?

Your opinion matters.

Review this book on your favorite book site, review site, blog or your own social media properties and share your opinion with other readers!

Be sure to connect with us at:
Harlequin.com/Newsletters
Facebook.com/HarlequinBooks
Twitter.com/HarlequinBooks